THE WITNESS PARADOX

The Witness Paradox

Copyright © 2018 by Tannhauser Press

Hardback ISBN: 979-8-43640-781-4
Paperback ISBN: 979-8-89719-030-0

Hardback Art and graphic layout by
Luca Oleastri and Paola Giari
Copyright © 2018 by Rotwang Studio
Edited by Jessica Johnson and Martin Wilsey
Published by Tannhauser Press

CONTENTS

DEDICATION

This book is dedicated to the librarian that took time out in 1972, at the Richmond Library in Batavia NY, to talk with me about Jules Verne, Albert Einstein and time travel. I wish I could remember your name.

When I get a time machine, I will thank you in person.

FOREWORD

I have always been fascinated with stories about time travel. In my youth I consumed books and movies and comics and television shows that involved time travel.

In high school, I remember long conversations with my Physics teacher, Mr. Will, regarding the science of time. My brain was on fire as I grew to realize the implications of $E=MC^2$ and time. The nature of relativity and the illusion of time.

In 1979 at college, after reading The Dead Zone by Stephen King, I read The Dancing Wu Li Masters by Gary Zukav and Godel, Escher, Bach by Douglas Hofstadter. By then my friends were sick of me trying to explain new physics after drinking too many pitchers of beer at the Field House.

"Shut up and write a science fiction novel."

Thirty five years later I took their advice.

Thanks Tom, Chaz, Bob, Jer, Phelp and Jimbo for putting up with me. Here is your first installment on time travel from me. With luck, and time, there will be many more.

Martin Wilsey
Managing Editor
Tannhauser Press
www.tannhauserpress.com

I got to Joey's Café early as usual. It was part of my Sunday morning ritual. Get up early, make coffee and read the week's submissions for the writers group. Relax a bit with my cat before I head out to Joey's.

It was hauntingly empty again this morning. I was the only one here at 9:36 am. As I sipped my coffee and munched on my bagel sandwich, I looked over the first submission titled *The Rescue*.

This was just an outline with a few details that we were going to brainstorm. It was always fun to brainstorm a topic. The group usually got really into it. It was a time travel story set in the present, where a time traveler is stranded and is trying to alert his partners in the future to come and pick him up.

I was personally interested in this piece because for the longest time I had been struggling with a time travel story.

"Morning, Marty," John said as he took his usual spot around the square table. "How goes?"

"So far, so good," I replied as usual. "I'm here and there's coffee."

The twelve seats around the table began to fill quickly. People set down their laptops or notebooks and went up to get coffee or food. Shea was even here today, and she waved from the direct opposite corner of the table.

"Morning, human," Dave said, beating me to it. He was the eleventh person there. He also dropped off his Mac and went in search of soda.

Penny Morris was the last to arrive, and she sat next to me on a corner of the table. She was always really shy in the group, an obvious introvert.

"Morning, Penny," I said. "How are you this fine day?"

She nodded rapidly and averted her eyes as she took a notebook and pencil from her satchel. The carry strap was diagonal across her shoulders and the bag rested in her lap.

I could see her hands were shaking as she fidgeted with her pencil. I don't know why but I looked at her closely then. She was fit. She was older than she seemed. I initially thought she was in her mid-twenties, but now reassessed her to be in her mid-thirties. She had subtle crow's feet at the corners of her eyes, and her hands just seemed… older. She had long, plain brown hair she kept in a classic single thick braid. She wore baggy sweatshirts most of the time with nerdy logos. Today it was Calvin and Hobbes exiting a TARDIS.

I think she caught me staring at her chest. I think I blushed.

Liz brought the meeting to order as we had four items to review. "First up, Penny has an outline for a story that she'd like to brainstorm with us. Penny, start with a general overview of what you are looking for."

I'm not sure anyone could see it but me, she swallowed hard before she spoke. "Well, this is a time travel sci-fi story. The story begins with the protagonist stranded in the past because of an accident that destroyed his time machine. He has to figure out how to get a message two hundred years into the future."

"If I were a time traveler I would have contingency plans," Bill said. "Like if I don't show up by 2 pm, go back and pick me up at this pre-determined location and time."

"He could just put an ad in the classifieds of the Washington Post," John said, "…that would list a day, time, and location. With some predefined verbiage."

"That's a Robinsonade trope," Bill added.

"What if there was a series of wars and the Internet was destroyed. No records like that," Penny said.

"Time Wars?" I asked.

"No, just conventional wars," Penny quickly answered. "Lots of EMP kills most of the computers. And nukes and bioweapons kill the people. Half the world population. Most paper only lasts about one hundred years."

"Is this guy trying to stop the war?" Liz asked.

"No…" Penny paused. "He is a historian. To him, the war was in the far past. He was sent back to study a turbulent time in history."

"Can time travelers in your story change the past?" Shea asked. "Like *Back to the Future* or is the past fixed? Ever see *The Time Tunnel*?"

"Yeah," Dave said. "Those guys never learned. Nothing they did could ever change the past. Sometimes they caused it."

"You remember that episode on the *Titanic* where…" The group started to talk about the variations in time travel tropes, themes, and stories. Multiple conversations broke out in laughter.

I noticed Penny looked like she was going to cry. Quietly, just to her, I asked, "Are you OK?"

"I have a friend where I'm from that loves your books," she said in a whisper. "You ever consider writing a time travel novel?"

The conversation got loud for a minute. "You can use a time-turner to save Buckbeak but not Dumbledore?"

"Yes," I said. "I have an outline now."

"What if in that book you mentioned a specific place, day and time?" Penny leaned in. "You know, where the protagonist gets rescued."

"A real place and time?" I asked.

"She might know your books survived and someone might recognize it as a message in a bottle and go check it out."

I was looking at her closely again. She didn't look away this time. I noticed she said *she*.

"*Time After Time* was the best," Kathleen inserted.

"Was that the Jack the Ripper one or the Chris Reeves one?" Jeff asked.

"*Somewhere in Time* was the Chris Reeves movie," Bill said.

***

I observed Penny staring across the room. Two men walked into the café. They looked like they were pressed from the same mold. Each had short haircuts and a Tom Selleck mustache. Both wore sunglasses, polo shirts, one red and one blue, a size too small. Plus matching mom-jeans that had not been in style for twenty years. They seemed out of place in several small details.

I gazed out the broad window wondering if I might see something unusual.

No one noticed them as time travel paradoxes had taken over the heated conversation. Movie and book references were flying as usual when a good topic had been launched.

"Ms. Morris," the one on the right said as the other scanned the room, "are you alright?"

"Yes. Yes, I am," she said. Her eyes began to fill with unshed tears that she blinked away. She looked into my eyes then.

She stood and packed her notebook in her bag. She spoke to the table. "My ride's here," Penny said smiling brightly. "I think that's enough to get started."

It was then I realized she was talking about me getting started.

She laid her hand on my shoulder. "It was an honor meeting you." And she kissed me on the cheek. The two men followed her out like perfectly trained Rottweilers.

I looked at my watch and noted the date and time.

My mind was on fire.

THE WITNESS PARADOX

Tanan awoke to the ringing in an instant. He grabbed the phone and said his name.

General McCarran's voice asked, "Can you be at Apex by 2300 hours?"

"What time is it?" Tanan looked at his watch.

As his eyes came into focus on the time, his superior answered, "2225 hours."

"I'll leave in five."

He quickly used the bathroom, threw on his jumpsuit and boots, hopped in the jeep and drove. Past dunes and desolation he arrived at a high chain-link fence with barbed wire across the top, angled outward. His jeep hummed to a halt at the entrance where two guards stood watch by a small tower. He showed his badge mechanically and they waved him in, recognition on their faces.

Above ground, Apex was a bland, unadorned one-story building. It resembled barracks or a low-end community college that was abandoned before completion. He drove around to the side where a garage door opened. The jeep rolled slowly in.

The garage door closed. The concrete ground tilted to a 30% grade and merged onto a curved ramp. He held the brake lightly while the vehicle descended. The ramp gradually flattened out into a plain. By the faint lights from the back of his vehicle, he could see the concrete that he'd descended upon lifting up again. He was in the underground parking and found an empty space in the section designated for operatives.

There were other cars, mostly transport vehicles that served as shuttles for the employees at Apex. Few people drove their personal vehicles directly to the facility. Usually they parked at Muroc Air Force Base, thirteen miles north. But Tanan hadn't caught a shuttle for years. He was expected to report direct.

He left the jeep and swiped his badge at the building's entrance. The door opened into a hallway that led to a metallic door. A marine sat at a desk behind bulletproof glass. The marine nodded, picked up a phone, said something inaudible and then waved toward the metallic door. It slid open, revealing General McCarran, silver-haired, robust and smiling.

"Good to see you, Tanan."

"Good to be seen. What's going on?"

The door slid shut behind them as they walked.

"Snafu. Visser Corp. Your clearance is being upgraded. You've climbed from 5 to 6."

"Yes, sir."

Together they boarded an elevator. There were no numbers on it, only a small scanner. General McCarran waved his badge and spoke. "Level 6."

Nothing happened. Tanan glanced at his superior.

"It's already upgraded," said the general. "Just wave and request."

Tanan waved his badge and said, "Level 6." The elevator began its descent. Had his clearance not been already upgraded, it would have stayed put. The computer that operated the elevator could tell by their weight that there were two of them, and both needed to have sufficient clearance.

Tanan remembered when he'd first been used as an Apex op. Given Level 3 clearance, he'd been taken to the third floor down, underground. He'd asked how many floors the base had and been told three. When he gained Level 4 clearance, he'd asked the same question and been told four. He didn't bother asking when he received his Level 5 and didn't bother asking now. Tanan was known for a few things: efficiency and a penchant for smarmy quips. But he also knew when silence was best.

The sixth floor was just like the other floors he'd been to. A workplace. Apex held odd hours, but like any office or military base, most people worked between 0800 and 1700 hours. So he hadn't expected it to be quite so bustling with lab techs and scientists. They all looked tired, and had that frantic glare in their eyes, along with the frenetic twitch that signified sleep deprivation mixed with slow, building panic.

They went into what Tanan first assumed was a robotics laboratory. He noticed several blueprints hung on the walls, all for some sort of bodysuit. Abstruse mathematics and shorthand notes riddled the posters, with lines running to parts of the prototypes and designs, like labels. It was so far beyond his education as to be another language.

McCarran led him to a frazzled looking scientist hunched over a computer. The screen was a mess of hieroglyphics only advanced physicists could decipher.

McCarran spoke. "Novikov. Novikov!"

The scientist spun around in his chair. He was younger than forty, but looked like sleepless nights had aged him.

"This is Tanan," McCarran said.

Novikov glanced him up and down. "He's a good fit."

"Of course he is." McCarran beamed. "The suit was designed for him."

"Well that's fortuitous," mumbled Novikov, probably knowing luck had no part in it.

"He's here to clean up our mess. He's not a science guy. Keep it simple."

"What does he know?"

"I haven't told him anything."

Novikov gazed at Tanan. "Do you know anything about the Casimir effect?"

"He doesn't need to know any of that shit," said McCarran, clearly about to lose his patience. "Give it to him simple, Novikov."

Novikov skipped to the point. "If I just jump into this, will you believe it?"

"Why not?" said Tanan. "I get paid the same either way."

"Do you know about the Visser Corporation?"

"I know enough."

McCarran interrupted. "We need you to infiltrate the facility again. Get whatever you can find. Something they're working on."

Tanan nodded.

"Navikov here can fill in some gaps if he ever gets around to it."

Navikov asked, "You know what traversable wormholes are?"

"No," Tanan replied. "Do I need to?"

"Visser Corp developed a huge underground room that doesn't allow anything in, short of neutrinos. I'll spare you the complicated part..."

"Thank you."

"A person can go into the room, and with certain spacetime coordinates entered into a computer, he can walk out into the future. To him, maybe a moment has passed, but to the outside world, any given amount of time has gone by."

"The future… Can they go into the past?"

"No."

"How do you weaponize going into the future?"

Navikov shrugged. "People find ways to weaponize anything, it seems. And we're fairly certain they've hyperdeveloped the technology. It's not a room anymore. They've made it mobile."

Tanan nodded.

"There's more. We intercepted communications between one of our chief scientists and Visser Corp. She offed herself before we could determine what she knew, and what they know. The transmissions are in deep cipher."

"So they know what you know," Tanan surmised, "and you don't know what they know."

"Most likely."

Tanan looked to McCarran. "Why don't you send in the big guns? Private corporations can't play dirty spy games with the US military."

"Agreed," said the general. "But this is a sensitive issue we want dealt with tactfully."

"I hope you pay me as much as you pay your fancy lawyers."

"I'm pretty sure we pay you more."

"You have a ride set up for me?"

"Yes."

"That skeleton key still work for their building?"

"It should."

"I still haven't told you about the suit," said Navikov.

"So tell me about the suit," said Tanan.

"Come on then." Navikov gestured for Tanan and McCarran to follow. They left the lab and went into another one. The walls were lined with various prototypes of the suit. Navikov brought one out from a glass case and laid it on a table. It was a full bodysuit with booties, gloves, a hood, and a mask. There was a wristwatch on one sleeve, a simple utility belt that had a baton strapped to it, and a couple little cartridges on either side of a bronze box the size of a cell phone. There was a red button with a safety cover attached the box.

"It goes on pretty easily, like a jumpsuit. Like the one you're wearing," Navikov said to Tanan.

"What's it do?" Tanan asked.

"The suit is connected to this device here." Navikov touched the bronze box. "It communicates your spacetime coordinates. And it protects you from the external elements."

"So what's the device do?"

"It's the TM, Temporal Manipulator. From the viewpoint of the user, it slows a second into a half hour. For about a minute, everything around you stops completely. Gradually, very gradually, things start moving again, and by the time a half an hour is up, in your perception, the world and you are back in sync."

"Now that's a weapon," said Tanan, impressed. "Stop time." He was at a loss for words. "So I put on the suit and time stops?"

"You don the suit and press the button on the waist belt. It has ten runs total." Navikov fondled the little cartridges. "These batteries are fully charged. On the wrist here is a timer. It begins counting from whatever the estimated time of operation is. It has a direct link to the batteries and tends to be accurate within a thousandth of a second. The perceived time outside of the suit would be about one second before the sequence is over."

"What happens if I press it twice?"

"Nothing. It won't permit that. It's too dangerous."

"What's its radius?"

"What?"

"How far does it extend? I mean, if I use it, does it just affect the people in the same room? Or does it extend to a city block or farther?"

"It doesn't extend beyond you. You're the only one affected. Nothing else is. Think of it like it's a super suit that gives you speed. And you gradually slow down until you're just regular again. Does that make sense?"

"Yeah, that makes sense. I like it." With a glance in the general's direction, Tanan added, "Sir, I believe you should continue paying this man, despite his personality."

"I've come to the same conclusion," McCarran replied.

Navikov went on. "So you understand you'll be moving at an incredible speed, relative to your surroundings. Don't remove your mask. When it's in operation, don't allow any portion of your body to be exposed. Don't breathe the outside air. Think of the external world as completely hostile."

"What happens with the outside air?"

"You can swim, right?"

"Uhuh."

"Can you swim if the water is frozen?"

"The air freezes?"

"It's not that simple, but in effect, yes. The suit's mask will acclimate the outside air to your relative temporal disposition. Take it off and breathing will be very uncomfortable. We've been through all this with rats, rabbits, monkeys and dogs. It turns out best when the suit covers the entire body."

"You got these for dogs, huh?" Tanan joked. "So if your scientist girl was giving secrets to Visser, they might have a suit as well."

"Be prepared for that. The real worry is that they have something we don't."

McCarran broke in. "We're trying to determine what Miss Verch knew and what she gave up to Visser Corp. We have reason to believe someone at Visser might be unscrupulous enough to sell it on the black market, despite our previous interventions."

Tanan nodded. "I'm sorry I'm stuck on the possibility, but what if they can go into the past?"

"You can't," said Navikov in firm tones.

"Can't? But we don't know."

"We do know. The past is fixed."

"You sure?"

"Traveling backward is impossible."

Tanan was unconvinced.

"One of three things happens if we actually could go into the past," Navikov explained. "Either you enter into a separate, undetermined timeline which sprouts into existence the moment you arrive and has no effect on our timeline. Or, no matter what you do, the trajectory of events remains the same. Go back to kill Hitler, and the past simply won't let you do it. Your gun misfires, his bodyguards take you out. Or maybe you can't physically interact with the past. You're like a ghost. A passive observer."

"That could work for spies," Tanan mused. "Invisible observer…"

"Yeah, if it were possible. But it's not. Like falling up. You can't change the laws of physics. You have to work within them."

"Maybe."

"You don't know what a traversable wormhole is and you're going to argue with me on this? I'm not gonna argue with you on how to…do whatever it is you do…"

"Fair enough."

"The past is fixed."

"Fine. Lemme try this thing on."

The suit fit Tanan perfectly and didn't constrict his movement. It was flexible and probably only weighed twenty pounds. He'd carried sixty when he was in the military, so the extra weight was nothing to him, so long as it added some other advantage.

"Feels good. Easy to move in."

"The suit won't restrict movement, but its function will," said Navikov.

"It changes when it's turned on?"

"No…but…"

"Is it bulletproof?"

"It isn't designed to be."

"What about fire? Water?"

"It can withstand high fluctuations of temperature. Don't use it as a shield in a firefight."

Tanan handled the baton.

"That's your weapon," Navikov said. "It's also designed to withstand the elements and has a direct connection to the TM."

"Run outta money by the time you got to the weapon?"

"That wasn't cheap. A projectile is problematic."

"A sword would've been cooler."

"This should be all you need."

Tanan shrugged, grinned, and nodded with approval. "I like it." He caught sight of Navikov's darkening expression. Tanan smiled. "What's the matter?"

Navikov stared at him, then addressed the general. "He's going to fuck this up."

"Excuse me?" said Tanan.

"You're in over your head," Navikov spat.

McCarran took it in stride. "Navikov, you're in charge of your team, but you're not in charge of operations like this. Do you have a better person for the task?"

Navikov clenched his fingers into fists. "He doesn't have a grasp of the implications…"

"Who gives a fuck?" said McCarran.

"I do. And you should too. Gorillas are strong, but what would happen if you gave one a gun?"

"You're serious?" Tanan said.

"I'm completely serious. A gorilla would be nice to have on your side in a fight. But it wouldn't understand the consequences of a firearm. That's why we don't train gorillas to be soldiers. They're too stupid."

"He's right about the gorillas, sir," Tanan said. "I met some in Africa. Lousy soldiers. Disorganized and sloppy."

McCarran grinned. "Anything else you need to tell Tanan about the suit?"

"No."

"Thank you, Navikov."

"Sir, may I have a word with him?" Tanan asked.

The general sighed. "A word."

Tanan didn't mind getting philosophical. "Navikov? You can sit all day pondering shit and making new toys, but your inventions, your discoveries…they're here to give one tribe an advantage over another. It's tribe versus tribe, you understand? And the strong determine which direction mankind's gonna advance. You make weapons. Someone needs to use them."

"That's how a soldier sees it," said Navikov, keeping his voice even.

"The brain needs hands," Tanan said, and before Navikov could say anything, he added, "and sometimes reflex needs to override thought. Otherwise, we act too late."

"It's time," said McCarran. "Take off the suit."

Navikov packed it in a small briefcase and gave Tanan the code to its lock.

McCarran escorted him to the above ground landing zone where a Huey awaited him. It transported him across state lines where ground transport met him in a clearing atop a small mountain peak.

The escort vehicle was a black six-seater SUV. Two men armed to the nines sat in front, and two sat in the back. All were large, burly security operatives, sub-contractors hired for jobs just like this, as well as more significant, more convoluted tasks overseas. Tanan had lived, fought alongside, and worked with men like this for over fifteen years. He always preferred working alone, but he was comfortable in the company of men like this.

He sat in the back, and the two back there sat facing him. As the SUV drove through winding country roads, a bearded, modern-day Viking asked him, "What're we doin' here boss?"

"You don't know the plan?" Tanan said.

"Don't know shit. They call us out here, tell us to take you into this place, tell us you're in charge."

His partner, a hefty African American, smiled, revealing a missing front tooth. "Said we're at your disposal, is what they said."

Tanan smiled back. "I appreciate the help. You guys are here for the same reason you're always around. In case things go to hell."

"Yeah. Why you here?" asked the Viking.

"Same reason I'm always around. Cuz someone fucked up." Then he realized he should probably introduce himself. "I'm Tanan."

"Busch," said the Viking.

"O'Ryan," said the other.

With introductions made, Tanan began to explain the mission. "We'll arrive about a mile from the site. Your driver and his shotgun remain with the vehicle. You two hike in the rest of the way with me. I have some experience with the terrain. Forest, nothing treacherous. Once we're in view of the building, you hang back and wait while I go in. When I come out, we go back to the vehicle, back to the LZ, and then I leave in the helo."

"What's the security like?" asked Busch.

"Private security. Typically two men of your caliber but out of practice. Other than that, it's your basic mall security with a handgun."

They nodded.

"Sounds like you just need a ride," said O'Ryan.

"Hopefully."

After that, the men joked amongst themselves and Tanan mostly kept quiet. Shortly after they arrived at the designated point. They hiked until they came within sight of a clearing, with a building inside of a high fence.

"Here's good," said Tanan. "Ideally this is gonna be silent. No gunfire. No noise."

"Copy."

He punched in four numbers on the briefcase and it popped open. He unzipped the jumpsuit he was currently wearing and then stepped into the new one. It was black. The hood came over his head and covered his face with a mask that was not as bulky as a gas mask, but not quite stylish enough to give him the real superhero look. Maybe a supervillain.

The security ops didn't say anything, just watched.

"If you'll excuse me," Tanan said. "I'll be back before you know it."

He ducked behind some trees beyond their sight. He pressed the button on his waistband. He could feel the change instantly. It was unnerving, a jolt that almost made him sick, like the first time he'd descended in a plane fast enough to achieve zero G. Some guys got motion sickness, but it was the weightlessness that had frightened him. This was the same sensation, that sensation of losing something he'd always existed within.

The wind had barely been a breeze, but it was gone. The little movements all around him had ceased. A forest is not silent, not motionless, and yet suddenly, this one was. It was like looking at a painting while standing in a vacuum.

Moving wasn't as bad as wading through water, but there was more resistance than usual, like a soundless wind was blowing against him in any direction he moved. Perhaps it took the air more time to get out of his way.

He pushed himself through, passing by Busch and O'Ryan. They were statues, utterly still.

He stalked as swiftly as possible through the clearing. Visser probably had security cams all over the place but would they record him? Was he moving so fast he'd register as a blur? He wasn't sure what the video would show.

He arrived at the front gate. The border around the building was made of steel and concrete, but the gate was tall iron. He'd already surmised he could climb it. When he grabbed it, it gave slightly, which made him uneasy. Yet he didn't have any problem ascending the iron spears and was careful not to get caught on the pointed tips at the top before he slid down to the other side.

He went to the front entrance. Apex had armed him with a skeleton badge that had a nifty way of overriding security systems like this. He slid it through, but nothing happened. For a moment he imagined Visser had upped their security but then remembered time was frozen.

He took a walk around the building. Before he'd gone far, he found an open bay with a black sedan and two men in suits, armed detail, with Visser himself. Visser was in his mid-forties, but a force in the world of weapons tech. The military loved him—when they could control him.

Visser practically lived on site, so it made sense he'd be here. It was particularly fortuitous he'd been either coming or going. It left him perfectly exposed.

Tanan hadn't been sent to kidnap Visser, but improvisation was vital. And no one knew more than Visser. Bringing him home for a quick conversation might be the prize trophy, or it might piss off the higher-ups. Tanan was willing to take the risk.

He pushed through the air and took hold of Visser's coat, giving it a tug toward the sedan. The sleeve came off in his gloved hand, melting like tissue in water, except in slow motion. Perplexed, he took hold of Visser's wrist but released as soon as he saw how the flesh was torn by his touch. The partially disintegrated sleeve cloth remained in the air, unable to fall.

It was velocity, pure and simple. He was flying around like a comet, and anything he touched would be devastated by his speed. It presented a conundrum. He couldn't move Visser. He would have to wait until time began to speed up again—or he slowed down.

The watch read 12:23.

He took the keys from the hand of one of the armed bodyguards, carefully. The only damage done was a little skin tear. He got into the sedan thinking he would start the car but doubted he could move the key slowly enough. It would probably snap. So he set it on the dash and got out of the car.

This weapon had its drawbacks, he realized.

When time sped up enough for him to interact with it, those guards would shoot him dead. He considered giving them a smack across the head but imagined the blow would be tantamount to a slice from a samurai katana, and probably cauterize the wound as well. Killing was part of the job, but it didn't need to be overdone. Instead, he pointed the baton at one of the guards' chest, pushed in and felt it sink like a fencer's sword into cheese. He withdrew it and moved on to the second guard and did the same.

This suit was an assassin's dream.

It'd been twenty minutes.

He waited. Time ticked by slowly.

The cloth from Visser's sleeve was almost on the ground now. The guards' expressions hadn't changed. Gravity and Death, both slaves to time.

At twenty-eight minutes, the guards showed the faintest hints of recognition. Visser hadn't noticed anything yet, not even the burns to his wrist.

Tanan gently took hold of Visser's coat sleeves near the shoulders and pulled him back. Visser came much more easily now, and the material just tore a little. He began to fall, surprised by the tug. Tanan released him.

Twenty-nine minutes.

The guards' eyes widened and both their faces began to contort into grimacing horror. It happened with comical slowness, but it was starting to move faster. The watch hit thirty minutes, and everything was seamlessly back to normal. One guard leaned forward and clutched his chest. He fell to the ground, moments from death. The other buckled at the knees, eyes going blank and lifeless. He collapsed in a heap.

Probably burned right through an artery in that one, Tanan figured.

By then Visser had completed his fall. Tanan yanked him off the ground and to the car. He threw him in the passenger seat, slammed the door and strapped himself in. He snatched the keys from the dash and started the ignition.

Visser hadn't had time enough to make sense of it.

Tanan drove smoothly out of the bay, around the building and toward the front gate.

"What's the code?" Tanan asked.

Visser looked frantically at the burns on his wrist and then back at his captor with nearly crazed eyes.

"The code," said Tanan calmly. "To get through the front gate. Tell me quickly, or I'll kill you."

"4589."

Tanan slowed to a halt and punched in the code, and the gate opened. He drove through. After a little way, he parked and pulled out his hostage.

"Let's walk."

"Who sent you?"

"Who do you think?"

"How many of you are there?"

"You're funny with the questions," Tanan said as he marched the man up the hill, toward his security escort. He was just in sight of them when he knew something was wrong.

Busch spotted him and pointed toward the Visser building. Tanan looked and saw a man emerging from the gate on foot, wearing a full bodysuit very much like his own. It was blue instead of black, and otherwise, he didn't have time to notice any other variations. And the blue-suited man had his hand on his waist belt.

Tanan initiated the TM device. Everything around him froze, but the man in the bodysuit had vanished.

He looked to the security detail. They hadn't moved, rendered into statues for the moment. But the blue-suited man was between them, and after a second Tanan realized what had happened. This guy had the same weapon he had. He'd frozen time just a moment before Tanan had, and had stolen the advantage. He'd come up the hill, to here, and by the look of things, had used a baton, just like his own, to cut through the two mercenaries. Tanan could see a line through O'Ryan's body and saw the baton passing through Busch like a hot knife through butter.

Both men were frozen in their bellicose postures and would never know how or why the battle had ended for them.

Tanan drew his baton. He wasn't sure what he was up against, but they were on equal footing here, or so he thought.

The Visser operative sheathed his baton, slow and smooth.

"Looks like you and I shop at the same outfitters," said Tanan.

The man said nothing, his face hidden behind a sleek mask.

"Except your mask is cooler. Mine's kind of clunky." Tanan watched him, trying to figure out where this was going.

The Visser op reached behind his back. He was moving slowly, Tanan noticed. He noted the distance between them. He might be able to make it to the op in time to strike him down and pummel him with the baton, but it was safer to use his hostage to his advantage.

Tanan jumped behind Visser and placed the baton within inches of his throat.

The Visser op pulled a large gun from his back and held it in front of his chest without pointing it at anything in particular.

"You brought your blow dryer?" said Tanan. "We gonna do our hair and have a slumber party? Come on, man. Let's make a deal. Visser probably pays you well, but they can't protect you much longer. Be a patriot and fight for the good guys."

The Visser op glanced at his gun, punched a few buttons on the top. His movements were in slow motion.

"Careful with that thing," said Tanan, becoming tense.

The Visser man pointed the wide barrel at himself and pulled the trigger with his thumb. There was a humming sound and then nothing. The man was gone, leaving no trace.

"Shit."

Tanan looked at his watch. 01:33. He had a long time before he could do anything. He waited, the way a mouse in a wall waits when a cat is prowling around somewhere nearby.

The problem was he didn't know the rules of the game he was playing. It was a stark advantage in war to have weapons beyond the understanding of the enemy, but that went both ways. Much of the history of humankind was a game of superior versus inferior weapons technology. Tanan didn't like being on the primitive side. Whatever that blow dryer looking gun really was, it was making him uneasy.

He took that twitchy, watchful half hour to think about it. He could guess it had to do with time travel. It had made the other op invisible, but that was an illusion. Maybe he had teleported to another time and place. The frightening thing was knowing that when he appeared again, he could freeze time and cut Tanan in half with no warning whatsoever.

It was the most exhausting second he'd ever known.

Finally, time caught up with itself. The two mercenaries had a gory demise. Both had been sliced in half. As he'd figured, the wounds were cauterized, and their grotesque deaths were unnervingly bloodless.

Like a trigger finger, he kept at the ready to press that button on his waist belt at a moment's notice, knowing that a moment could be too late in this scenario. With the other hand, he grabbed Visser and pulled him along.

"What's the gun do?" he asked.

"You're out of your league, aren't you?"

"You're basically naked in the woods, Visser. I'd say you were out of your league."

"You won't kill me, will you?"

"Guys like you always sound so confident. Even at the very end, you just can't believe it. But no, not unless I have to. Between you and me, it's gonna be you, not me. Hopefully you know that much."

"Of course."

Tanan sensed someone behind him. He turned and saw the Visser op standing twenty yards away. Like two gunslingers, they stared at one another, each with his hand on his belt, finger near the button.

Tanan pressed it.

The Visser op was frozen, his hand on his own belt. Tanan had won. He started toward his opponent. Abruptly the Visser man unfroze, and he moved fast.

Tanan tried to do the math in his head. If the Visser op had frozen time a fraction of a second after he had, what would that mean? *The implications…*Navikov's words echoed cruelly in his head.

Tanan was too close to retreat. He had to attack. He charged toward the other op, baton drawn. The Visser man pulled his gun, but this time Tanan was already on him. He swung the baton toward the Visser man. The Visser op moved his hand out of the way with appalling swiftness. Without a pause, Tanan followed with a front snap kick to the man's groin, but the op merely stepped back to avoid it. Tanan swung at the man's clavicle, but again he sidestepped with inhuman speed. Tanan was not used to being bested this way.

The op stepped back, then spun around with a well-practiced heel kick that came so fast Tanan had no chance of blocking or evading it. It landed just below his armpit, and his diaphragm seized. He bent over and backed up.

The blue-suited op raised the strange gun and aimed it at Tanan.

"Wait," said Tanan, trying to catch his breath. Anything to buy time.

The op stared at him, his face a comic-book character's mask. He backed away, then looked down and punched a couple buttons into the gun. His movements were in fast-forward. He took aim at Tanan again.

"What did you just dial into there?"

"Coordinates," he said in a high-pitched voice, like a recording played at high speed.

Tanan had his breath back but pretended to be hurt. He put out a hand and said, "Please, wait." Then suddenly, he made a lunge. But the op pulled the trigger and the gun hummed in a higher pitch than before. Tanan might have made it, all things being equal, but they weren't.

Tanan landed on the ground. The op was gone.

"Son of a bitch."

He stood, glanced around. The forest he'd been in wasn't there. He was in a tropical jungle. He and time were in sync again. He could tell by the soft wind and the overwhelming sounds of the environment. It was hot, muggy, humid. And it was day.

Then the noises around him changed, and he heard something stomping, like an elephant trampling toward him. He backed up, assaulted by the sound of the jungle being torn asunder to clear a path for a giant.

The jungle parted, and a monster emerged, its enormous jaws open wide, its long neck stretching as its head raged toward him.

Tanan punched the button.

The thing stood there motionless, two clawed feet on the ground, the other two in midair, about to land. The creature had a thick coat of shimmering, green-brown fur. Its eyes were brilliant yellow. If it resembled anything, it would have to be a wolf. But it was at least six feet tall, with a hairless rat's tail that appeared prehensile.

After examining the beast, Tanan drew his baton and sliced off its head, which remained on its neck for the time being.

Tanan marched off, bewildered, unable to fully process his defeat.

That's how they weaponized it, he thought. *By blowing the enemy into prehistory.*

Time gradually caught up, and he was hiking through the lush, horrifying jungle in real time. Everything was nightmare sized. Insects were huge. He saw a dragonfly the size of a cat, a grub like a football, and at one point caught sight of an arachnoid crab, big as a steering wheel, clinging motionless to a tree. He was too terrified to touch anything.

He wandered for almost a day before he came upon what could only be called a camp. He kept his distance and watched a group of around thirty hominids huddled in little cliques. They resembled some mad scientist's splicing experiment gone awry. Like a mix between human and lemur. Small, furry, with huge black bulbs for eyes. Yet they interacted with intelligence.

Were these his ancestors?

And then a thought haunted him.

The past is fixed.

If the Visser op had been able to use the gun to go back in time, why not defeat Tanan before he'd infiltrated the building? When he'd used it on himself, he appeared to disappear, probably going a few seconds into the future. The only reason he wouldn't go back in time is if he couldn't.

Which meant the other op had sent him forward. That wolf wasn't some ancestor of modern canines. It was a descendant.

"This is what you get when you give guns to the gorillas," he said, realizing Navikov's point.

One of the lemur people looked in his direction, its big, bulbous eyes discerning movement. It was the largest, with two females grooming its silver fur. It homed in on Tanan and swatted the females away.

Tanan stood up.

The lemur thing stood too, but was apparently uncomfortable as a biped, and quickly squatted again. A few of its tribe squealed and barked articulately, bouncing and scurrying, both frightened and threatening. Then they promptly spoke in grunts and chitterings to one another.

Tanan had nowhere to go. He started toward his descendants. Some fell back while others postured, ready for a fight. The one that spotted him first barked like a dog and tensed its muscles. Tanan pushed the button and everything stopped.

After this run, he had five TM sequences left.

Time to adapt.

Professor Thomas Arbor exited the elevator onto the third floor of Becker Hall at the University of South Carolina at Charleston.

From the bench along the far wall, a tall, lean man of about fifty with an athletic build and square handsome features stood. As he stepped forward, the man asked, "May I have five minutes of your time, Professor?"

"I'm afraid I don't have five minutes," Professor Arbor replied, lifting his bulging, worn leather briefcase. "I've got papers to grade. It's the end of the semester."

"Please, sir, I seek only five minutes," the man pleaded. "I have a proposal that I believe will greatly interest you."

The professor asked, "Proposal? What kind of proposal?"

"It involves Jesus," the man said. "The chance to learn the truth about him. Did he exist? Was he crucified?" After a pause, he added, "Was he the son of God?"

As the professor gave a dubious frown, the man said, "Look, I'm no lunatic. I'm a scientist, like you. And I'm telling you, I've discovered a way to learn the truth about Jesus. What do you have to lose to hear about it except five minutes?"

Professor Arbor considered the man a long moment, before unleashing a sigh. "Alright. Five minutes."

***

"My name is Major Jack Stafford, retired Army," the man began.

He was sitting on an armless chair in Professor Arbor's cramped office. The professor sat listening on a squeaky leather swivel chair, behind an undersized desk cluttered with papers, professional journals and textbooks.

"Before retiring," the major went on, "I participated in a top-secret project involving the use of psychic powers in espionage and combat operations. My specialty became remote viewing, the ability to observe things at some distant location—enemy combatants, weapons systems, hostages, that sort of thing. In fact, I got quite good at it. Six terrorists owe their deaths to my ability to remote view their hiding places.

"Anyway, during the project, I began experimenting with the cousin of spatial remote viewing—temporal remote viewing. Rather than viewing a present location to find a person or a thing, temporal remote viewing allows one to observe a past event." With a smile, he added, "The ability to do that, I call historinautics. And the person, like myself, who can do it, a historinaut.

Major Stafford continued, "But, the Army saw little use for it. You see, historinautics works only backward in time. One can observe the past, but not the future." He smirked again. "Something must have already happened in order to observe it, right?

"In addition to that," he went on, "a historinaut can only observe the past event, not participate in it. Like watching a movie, if you will. From the Army's perspective, what good was knowing what already happened without being able to change it?

"But I saw it differently. I saw a huge market in being able to witness a past event. Imagine the possibilities—a historinaut can solve crimes, determine the causes of accidents, answer historical mysteries, and so forth.

"So, I decided to retire from the Army and open the Institute of Applied Historinautics. Soon enough, I found that I was right. Temporal remote viewing has proven to be quite lucrative. People will pay handsomely to find out what really happened in the past."

Major Stafford reached forward and placed the thin paperback he'd been holding on Professor Arbor's desk. With a frown, the Professor picked it up. He inspected the cover. "*What Really Happened – The Assassination of President John F. Kennedy*, by Major Jack Stafford, Retired U.S. Army, with Alan R. Miller." The professor gave Major Stafford a halfhearted shrug.

"The book you're holding," the major explained, "presents a narrative of my temporal remote view of President Kennedy's assassination in Dallas on November 22, 1963. It reports how I got there, and of course, what I witnessed."

"And what did you witness?"

"As some have theorized," the major said, "there was more than one assassin. I saw three. One from the Texas Book Depository—though not Lee Harvey Oswald, who was indeed set up, a patsy. Another assassin from an office on the fourth floor of the building next door, the Dal-Tex Building. And the third behind a fence on what's known as the Grassy Knoll. So, yes, there was a conspiracy to kill the President. And from several subsequent remote views, I took to that time period, I was able to identify who those assassins were." Major Stafford leaned back, flashing a smug grin. "But to learn that, you'll have to read the book." After a sigh, he added, "Unfortunately, as I said, while I could remote view the President's assassination, I was helpless to prevent it."

"And Alan Miller," the professor asked, "who's he?"

"A journalist. Alan helped me write the book. I'd never written a book before."

After turning over the paperback and squinting at the back cover for a time, Professor Arbor tossed the book onto his cluttered desk. This is all very absurd, sir. Please, you've had your five minutes." He checked his watch. "More than five minutes."

The major held up his right hand, as if to stave off the professor's dismissal. "Look, I know it sounds crazy. But check out my credentials. I've helped solve several homicide cold cases for the police, and the detectives involved in those cases will vouch for my credibility, as will certain private clients I've helped learn the truth about a past event."

The professor gave this some thought. "But why should I do that, check out your credentials? What has any of this got to do with me?"

"It's got everything to do with you, Professor," the major said. "I want and need your help in conducting my temporal remote view to learn the truth about Jesus. First, to help me determine the precise spacetime coordinates where I'll be going. And second, to vouch for the historical accuracy of what I observe when I get there."

The professor snorted. "And then you'll write a book about it."

"Well, yes," the major replied. "My publisher wants me to write a series of these what really happened books. The Kennedy assassination book has sold quite well."

Though it sounded crazy, as the major had admitted, the chance of assisting the major in witnessing the events leading to Jesus' crucifixion, and what happened afterwards, on that first Easter Sunday, was almost too enticing to pass up. His entire academic and professional career and indeed his very life had been devoted to determining the details of those very events, blurred by time and marred by Christian theology. It was nearly impossible to tell what was fact and what was myth.

After a time, Professor Arbor said, "Let me think it over. Check out your credentials, as you've suggested. Then, I'll get back to you."

The major stood, reached into his pocket, fished out a piece of paper and set it on the professor's desk. "I've jotted down the names and numbers of three detectives and two private clients. Call them, hear what they have to say. And read my book. Then, call me, let me know. But please, I ask that you do so within the next two days."

"Two days?"

"I've booked a trip to Jerusalem for three days from today. If you're not going, I have a Professor Kruger lined up. You know him?"

"Kruger?" The professor narrowed his eyes. "Yes, I know him." Then he exhaled. "Why Jerusalem?"

"For the spatial coordinates. I not only need to know when in spacetime I'm going, but where. It was easy enough to remote view Dealey Plaza in Dallas fifty years ago, but, as you can appreciate, looking back two thousand years is quite another matter. But you, Professor, can provide me with the necessary details, the time coordinates, your estimate of the pertinent dates. And for the spatial coordinates, where in Jerusalem Jesus may have spent his final days. I need to see those places so I can focus upon them as they were two thousand years ago."

"I assume you know Aramaic," the professor said, "the language of Judeans and, of course, Jesus and his disciples in 30 A.D. I would think, should you really go there, you'll want to understand what Jesus is saying to his followers, his disciples, the Sanhedrin priests, and Pontius Pilate."

"I have a rudimentary knowledge," the major said. "I was hoping you would help me master it better during our trip to Jerusalem."

Professor Arbor again wondered whether he could believe this man and his crazy sounding proposal. Finally he said, "You'll have my answer tomorrow afternoon. And now, sir, I really must get to these papers!"

***

Major Stafford had booked two rooms at the New Imperial Hotel near the Jaffe Gate in the Old City of Jerusalem. For three days after checking in, Professor Arbor led him on a tour of the Old City. He took him to the locations where, based upon his research, he believed that Jesus and his disciples had visited in the days preceding Jesus's arrest, trial and crucifixion during the first week of April in 30 A.D. Each evening, the professor met with the major for a couple hours in his room to improve his grasp of Aramaic and prepare him for the sights and sounds of ancient Jerusalem.

On the last night of their stay, the major opened a bottle of Glenlivet twenty-five-year-old malt scotch. He poured the scotch into two glasses and handed one to Professor Arbor, who sat in an armchair in the corner of the room next to the bed. The major held up his glass.

"To witnessing the last days of Jesus," he toasted. Major Stafford took a sip from his glass and savored the taste of the scotch. The professor winced after his sip.

"It's an acquired taste," said the major. Then he asked, "If he is the son of God, do you think he'll realize I've come back from two thousand years in the future to watch him?"

"Neither you nor I believe that Jesus is the son of God," the professor replied. After another sip, he added, "Paul of Tarsus made him that. Jesus desired only to be accepted as the messiah foretold by the prophets so he could establish Yahweh's Kingdom on earth."

After a time, Major Stafford said, "You know, Professor, you could do it."

"Do what?"

"Become a historinaut. All it takes is extreme concentration. And practice. Lots of practice. But anyone can learn how."

The major set his drink on the night table, strode over to the closet, fetched his suitcase and carried it to his bed. Upon opening it, he dug for a moment under his clothes before pulling out a thin booklet, then walked over and handed it to the professor. Professor Arbor squinted at the title, *Guide to Applied Historinautics.*

"Contains everything you need to know about temporal remote viewing," said the major. "I wrote it."

The professor flipped through the booklet then held it up for the major to take back.

"No, keep it," Major Stafford said. "Someday, perhaps you'll want to use it yourself. Go back in time. See Jesus."

***

Ten days later, Professor Arbor sat before the wide desk of Sheila Renfrew, the Dean of the Department of Religious Studies. She was a white-haired, stout middle-aged woman who looked especially displeased that morning. A newspaper of some kind was opened before her.

Professor Arbor had received the dean's email late yesterday afternoon directing him to appear for this meeting. It had provided no inkling what was to be discussed, only that he "promptly appear."

"You've been away," Dean Renfrew began. She bent forward and peered at him from over her gold-rimmed spectacles. "To Jerusalem, I understand. I thought you were going there on a dig in late June."

"I am," the professor replied. "This visit was entirely personal."

"Did your trip have anything to do with this article?" She offered him the newspaper. After taking it, Professor Arbor saw that it was the latest edition of The Global Inquirer, a supermarket tabloid. He sat glowering as he scanned the two pages to which the newspaper had been opened, reading an article entitled, "Historinaut to Visit Jesus," with the byline, "Alan Miller." On page one of the article was a large photograph of a grinning Major Stafford. Inserted within its frame was a smaller photograph of a serious looking man—him—copied from the faculty directory of the college's website. Finally, the professor looked up.

"I take it you are the same Professor Arbor referred to in the article?" the dean asked.

With a shrug he said, "Yes, of course. That's my photograph."

Dean Renfrew signaled for him to return the paper.

"So, the article is correct in its report," the dean continued, "that you've agreed to assist this, this histor..." She glanced down at the article to find the word.

"Historinaut," the professor filled in.

"Yes, historinaut. You've agreed to assist him in traveling back to the time of Jesus?"

"Well, not traveling back in time," Professor Arbor corrected. "He doesn't step into a time machine or anything. He remote views, he says. Focuses his mind to see the past, like watching a video of the event. I'm merely assisting him do that on my own free time with no affiliation with the university or this department."

"But being a professor here," replied Dean Renfrew, "as noted in the article, does draw this university and this department into it. I can tell you, Thomas, several trustees are most displeased by this. And Dean Wilkerson is unhappy."

"But this man," Professor Arbor said, "has impressive credentials. He's helped solve several homicides. I've spoken with the detectives on those cases who've confirmed that the details he furnished were not only instrumental in solving them but could only have been known by someone who witnessed the actual murders. Imagine that, the terrible ability of being able to focus on a murder and watch it happen. That's what each of these detectives believe he must have done.

"And according to several experts," the professor went on, "the details on the Kennedy assassination provided in his book had the ring of authenticity as well. What I mean to say, Dean Renfrew, is that I didn't agree to participate in this project on a whim."

After a sigh, the Dean said, "Well, what's done is done. I summoned you here this morning merely to report the concerns of the trustees and Dean Wilkerson. As you say, your participation is personal. But remember, your contract forbids personal activities that bring disrepute upon the university."

Professor Arbor frowned. "Meaning what?"

"I leave the meaning to your discretion," Dean Renfrew replied. "It's still being deliberated. I felt obliged to let you know that. And perhaps, to dissuade your further participation."

Professor Arbor's frown deepened. He was angry now. Still, he stopped himself from blurting out that Dean Wilkerson and the offended trustees weren't offended by the prestige his books on the historical Jesus, *The Jesus Legacy* and *The True Founder of Christianity*, had brought the university. He took a deep breath. "I'll certainly take your admonition under advisement. Thank you."

With that, the professor stood and was about to leave when Dean Renfrew said, "There's one more thing you should know. It's in the article."

"Yes?"

"The Pope is sending an emissary to monitor the project." Staring down at the article, she read, "Cardinal Enrico Ginetti, head of the Vatican's Congregation for the Doctrine of Faith." She looked up. "As you know, that body is responsible for defending Catholic theology from attack."

With a nod, the professor said, "Well, then, it should make the project all the more interesting."

"Or turn it into a full-blown circus," the dean replied. "You know, Thomas, your Major Stafford is a clever salesman. No matter what he claims to have seen, having you there, and a cardinal from the Vatican, will most certainly help him sell more books and obtain more clients."

"Perhaps," Professor Arbor replied. "Is there anything else, Dean?"

She shook her head and gave him a long exasperated look. She must have been wondering how it was that the most acclaimed professor in the department had so completely lost his senses.

***

The Institute of Applied Historinautics occupied an 800-square foot space. It was at the far end of a nondescript strip mall along a busy stretch of Orange Blossom Trail, just east of Orlando. The other spaces of the mall were leased to a nail salon and spa, a take-out Chinese Restaurant, a Disney knock-off outlet, a sub shop, and a smartphone service store.

At nine that morning, Professor Arbor walked into a small waiting room with a vacant receptionist's kiosk at the far end. As the professor entered, he spotted the major, who was now sporting a sleek, black tracksuit. There were also two other men he didn't recognize. A stout man in his early seventies in a traditional black cassock, who the professor assumed must be Cardinal Enrico Ginetti. Which meant the other man, in the jeans and tee shirt, was Alan Miller. The major flashed the professor a welcoming grin. "Ah, we're all here." After brief introductions, Major Stafford gestured to the open door next to the kiosk. "This way gentlemen."

They followed him down a short, narrow hallway into a conference room with an oval wooden table. Upon entering, Major Stafford walked to the far end of the table before a curtained window and offered chairs to his guests. Cardinal Ginetti sat next to Professor Arbor along the center of the table nearest the door, while Alan Miller took a seat across from them.

"Gentlemen," Major Stafford began, "welcome to the Institute of Applied Historinautics. It's not much, I know. But the work done here is what matters.

"It's my hope," he went on, glancing at Professor Arbor and Cardinal Ginetti, "that you will keep an open mind. I assure you that I have no preconceptions as to what I might find during this temporal remote view. I only seek historical truth.

"To recap," Major Stafford continued, "I will remote view the last days of Jesus to confirm, first of all, his existence. Then, if he was crucified by the Romans at the behest of the Sanhedrin priests. And finally, if he truly rose from the dead on the Sunday after his crucifixion." The major looked at his guests and asked, "Any questions so far?"

After Professor Arbor and Cardinal Ginetti shook their heads, the major continued. "This morning, I shall attempt to remote view April 3, 30 A.D., a Wednesday." He turned to Professor Arbor. "Is that correct, Professor?"

"Yes," the professor replied, "those are the time coordinates we agreed upon."

"And I will be going to the upper room of a guesthouse in the lower city, just north of the pool of Siloam," the major added.

With a mild Italian accent, the Cardinal asked, "Why there? And on Wednesday?"

"Because," Professor Arbor replied for the major, "that was where Jesus had his last meal with his disciples—a Wednesday, not a Thursday, as is traditionally accepted. And, from my research, it took place in 30 A.D., not 33."

Professor Arbor spent the next several minutes explaining the basis for selecting this date. All the while, the frown lines around Cardinal Ginetti's mouth deepened. He did not look convinced. After the professor had finished, the cardinal said, "Well, we shall see."

"In any event, that's where I'm going this morning." Major Stafford went on. "If the date is wrong, or the place, we can always adjust the spacetime coordinates." After pausing to catch his breath, he said, "Now, let me explain how a temporal remote view—or what I call a time trip—works."

Major Stafford pulled a chord, opening the curtain of the window behind him. It offered a view into the room next door. Immediately visible was a large, black, triangular tent in the corner against the far wall, and a cot next to it. Turning to them, the major explained, "The black tent is a deprivation chamber. Inside there's a float tank, an eight-by-four, five-foot-high pool. The tank has been filled with ten inches of water heated to skin temperature, 93.5 degrees Fahrenheit. Eight hundred pounds of Epsom salt have been poured into the water, enabling a human body to float.

"When the entrance flap of the tent is closed," he went on, "it's pitch dark inside. The tent is also soundproof. Once floating in the pool, I will feel, see and hear nothing. And after concentrating on the place and time I wish to visit, I'll enter a trancelike state and be transported to the targeted event, blurry at first, but soon enough, it'll come into focus.

"In my experience," the major continued, "the typical time trip can last no more than an hour and a half to two hours, before the mind loses focus. The trance fades and the remote view ends. I wake up in the present.

"Another problem," the major said, "a time trip is linear. If I'm on the trip for an hour, I see what happens in that hour. To jump between multiple spacetime coordinates, I must awaken from the trance, then start over again. That, in my experience, is difficult to do.

"For viewing an event like the Kennedy assassination, or a cold case murder, that isn't a problem. I can view the entire event in a single trip. But for this event, observing Jesus over several days—from the Last Supper on

Wednesday, April third, to the first Easter, on Sunday, April seventh, will take several trips. Is that understood?"

Professor Arbor nodded, having already heard this explanation, while Cardinal Ginetti held a glum expression. For his part, Alan Miller slumped down in his chair with his eyes closed.

"You should also be aware," the major continued, "that I can normally take only one trip per day, as they are quite exhausting. After a trip, I'll be spent, requiring rest for the remainder of the day. Therefore, your monitoring of my remote views may take several days, though by my calculation, no longer than a week." He surveyed the room before asking, "Are there any questions before I begin?"

"During your, ah, time trip," Professor Arbor asked, "we wait here?"

"Yes," the major said. He nodded to the window. "There won't be much to see after I enter the deprivation tent and start the trip. As I said, I'll be remote viewing for between an hour or two." He gestured to a credenza along the far wall of the conference room. "There's coffee, donuts and water. Across the hall there's a restroom. I should have told you to bring reading materials. Sorry about that. Anything else?" He glanced at the cardinal. "Your Eminence?"

His arms still crossed over his chest, Cardinal Ginetti grunted, "No."

"Very well, then." The major cracked his knuckles. "Time to go."

The major left the room. Moments later, the professor, looking through the window, saw the major enter the room next door. The major unzipped his tracksuit, revealing a swimmer's thong underneath. After laying the tracksuit on the cot, he went over, crouched down and entered the deprivation tent through a triangular flap. A moment later, the flap closed. Presumably, the major was now floating face up in a bath of warm water, saturated with Epsom salt, commencing a time trip.

Professor Arbor and Cardinal Ginetti stood next to each other, peering through the window. After a time, Alan Miller said, "Might as well sit down and relax, gentlemen. Like the major said, there's not much to see."

Cardinal Ginetti turned to Miller and asked, "You believe that he can do this—see the past? That he witnessed the assassination of your President Kennedy? Or are you paid to believe it?"

"I'm a journalist," Miller replied. "Even if I work for a tabloid, I report the truth."

The priest laughed dismissively and lumbered over to his chair. After a moment, Professor Arbor sat in his.

"And you, Professor," the cardinal asked, "what do you believe?"

Professor Arbor thought for a moment, then said, "As a historian, I hope it's true. The ability to see the living Jesus, what he did, what he said, what happened to him. Things we can only guess at now."

"Only those without faith are left to guess," Cardinal Ginetti said. "I've read your books, Professor. Very interesting ideas, though wrong."

"My ideas are based on verifiable research," the professor replied in an even voice. "The work of countless scholars who agree that though Jesus existed, he was not the son of God. That he did not rise from the dead. Indeed, Jesus never claimed that. Those claims were created out of whole cloth by Paul of Tarsus, years after the event."

"Well, perhaps Major Stafford will prove your theories wrong," said the priest.

"Or your faith."

With a shrug, Cardinal Ginetti whispered, "Perhaps."

***

Nearly two hours later, Major Stafford stumbled back into the conference room. He plopped down onto a chair at the head of the table and spent the next minute or so staring down at it.

Finally, Professor Arbor asked, "Major, are you alright?"

When the major looked up with a weak smile and a short nod, Miller chimed in. "He'll be fine. He's always like this after a trip. He just needs a moment."

After a breath, the major said, "Thank you, Alan. Yes. Some rest."

"Can you at least tell us, Major?" Professor Arbor asked. "Did you see him? Jesus."

After a time, the major said, "Yes. I saw him."

A burst of air emitted from Cardinal Ginetti's throat, revealing his amusement and disdain. Ignoring this, Professor Arbor asked, "Where did you see him? "

"As you advised," the major said. "Having a meal with his disciples, in an upper room of a guesthouse in the lower city."

Professor Arbor clucked gleefully.

"Utter nonsense," the priest commented.

The major suddenly sagged, seeming barely able to hold his head up. "I'm sorry, gentlemen, but you must excuse me." With some effort, he glanced at Professor Arbor and Cardinal Ginetti. "Let me rest awhile, then I'll prepare a full report of my trip, what I saw. You'll receive it by email sometime this evening."

***

As promised, at about seven that evening in his hotel room, Professor Arbor received an email reporting the major's time trip. The professor was immediately impressed by the report's detailed description of the Judean homes and various other buildings from the period—the pale, whitewashed look of the fired-brick walls constructed from limestone and dolomite quarried from the hills around the Old City. The smells and sounds of daily life that the major described also seemed authentic—the aroma of baked breads and roasted grains and legumes and olive oil wafting out from the houses and stalls in city markets through the narrow streets. And the din of Judeans bustling about their daily tasks, even busier now on the eve of the coming Passover that Friday.

The major's description of the upper room where Jesus had his last meal with his disciples on Wednesday also seemed authentic—the grains, figs, pomegranates, unleavened bread and, of course, wine. But what impressed the professor most was Major Stafford's depiction of Jesus. It closely matched how he had imagined his appearance and manner of speaking based upon his countless hours studying the writings of St. Paul, the Gospels and other historical records going back two thousand years.

Missing from the major's report was the famous event, cited in the Gospels, that during the Last Supper, Jesus identified Judas Iscariot as his betrayer. But it's absence only served to enhance the professor's confidence in the report's authenticity. It had long been his opinion that if Jesus had been aware of Judas' betrayal, why would he have gathered with his disciples in Gethsemane, exactly where Judas knew he would be that night?

The major's failure to note that Jesus had given bread and wine to his disciples as the symbolic representation of his body and blood in a new covenant with God also comported with the professor's views of the historical Jesus. The symbolic drinking of blood would have been blasphemous for a Jew. Professor Arbor believed that this purported act on the part of Jesus was yet another invention of Paul of Tarsus in establishing a false Christianity.

According to Major Stafford, Jesus' meal with his disciples lasted slightly longer than an hour and a half. By that time, the major's head pounded as he tried to stave off his faltering concentration. He continued observing as Jesus and his disciples rose from their chairs behind a long table and began shuffling out the room and stumbling their way down a long, narrow stone pathway to the Garden of Gethsemane that made an excellent hiding place with its centuries old olive trees grown together forming a shadowy canopy. The major's report ended at this point, promising that he would visit the garden during his next trip to view Jesus's expected arrest as set down in scripture.

After his third reading of the report, Professor Arbor went to sleep more hopeful than ever that the major had indeed witnessed the living, breathing Jesus and his disciples sharing what was to be their last meal together. He was also excited as to what the major might observe during his successive time trips over the next few days, culminating in his observation of the first Easter Sunday.

***

At nine the following morning, Professor Arbor, Cardinal Ginetti and Alan Miller convened in the conference room of the Institute of Applied Historinautics. Standing at the head of the table before them, the major asked, "Are there any questions or comments regarding last night's report?"

"Interesting," Professor Arbor replied, not wanting to tip his hand by adding, *convincing* or *impressive.*

"I have none," grunted Cardinal Ginetti.

A bored, tired looking Alan Miller said, "None from me."

With a nod, Major Stafford said, "This morning I go back to the Garden of Gethsemane to witness Jesus' arrest."

The major's time trip that morning lasted only an hour and fifteen minutes and, when he returned to the conference room, he did not look as tired as he had the previous morning.

"Jesus was indeed arrested at Gethsemane," he announced. "And, though it appears he had no foreknowledge of it, Judas Iscariot did indeed betray him with a kiss. The forces that came out to arrest him were considerable. There were the leading priests, a detachment of the Temple guard, and a cohort of Roman soldiers. And Simon Peter—though Jesus and others called him Cephas—did indeed draw a knife and cut off the ear of the high priest's servant, Malchus, before Jesus interceded to prevent further resistance."

The major's report on Jesus' arrest arrived in Professor Arbor's email just after eight, and he was again favorably struck by its detail and accuracy. As he went to bed, the professor was more confident than ever that Major Stafford could indeed look back into time and was about to witness the most important event in human history.

***

Major Stafford's session the following morning lasted nearly three hours. When he stumbled into the conference room, Professor Arbor and Alan Miller had to help him into his chair at the head of the table. After catching his breath, the major said, "I performed multiple trips this morning." His voice was raspy, barely audible.

"What I viewed were Jesus' trials, his beatings, and his hanging on the cross." Stafford lowered his head and closed his eyes for a time. Finally, he looked up and added, "Though I had trouble remaining focused, I couldn't stop watching." He swallowed. "I had to watch Jesus die on the cross."

The major told them that as Jesus neared death, at just before three on Thursday afternoon, April 4, 30 A.D., he indeed called out, "Eloi, Eloi, Lama sabachthani? My God, my God, why have you forsaken me?"

A short time later, when Jesus appeared to have expired, the cross was lowered and the ropes around his hands and feet were untied. His lifeless body was given over to Joseph of Arimathea, a Sanhedrin priest, and several servants carried it to a cave not far away, near Golgotha, while accompanied by Jesus's mother, his lover, Mary Magdalene, and a sister. "And that's where I ended the trip," Major Stafford said, "as Jesus' body was placed in the tomb. For my next time trip, tomorrow morning, I will return to this same tomb at sunrise on Sunday, April 7, 30 A.D.—the first Easter Sunday. During that remote view, I hope to answer the question of whether Jesus truly rose from the dead—whether he truly is the son of God."

He staggered out of the conference room to the room next door and collapsed onto the cot.

***

The following morning, Professor Arbor was twenty minutes late getting from the hotel to the Institute. He hadn't slept well the night before, restless from anticipation. He woke at two a.m., got out of bed, powered up his laptop on the desk and spent the next hour re-reading the major's reports. They seemed credible, as if told by a man who had truly witnessed the Last Supper, Jesus's arrest and trial, his death on the cross and burial. But what he'd observe tomorrow morning was the big deal, information that might change history.

Having finally tired from reading the reports, Professor Arbor fished from his briefcase the guide for temporal remote viewing that the major had given him. He spent some time skimming through it and decided that with enough practice, he might indeed be able to do it—concentrate on a set of spacetime coordinates and then witness a past event.

The professor didn't climb back under the covers until almost four-thirty. He tossed and turned for a while longer until finally, he fell asleep. The alarm awakened him at eight, and he closed his eyes for a moment after turning it off. He woke with a start forty-five minutes later and scrambled out of bed to the shower. Now he was dreadfully late on the biggest day of his life.

***

When he pushed open the door to the conference room, two expectant faces turned to him.

"Oh, it's you," Alan Miller said. Miller added, "He's late—Major Stafford."

"Oh?" The professor sat in his usual chair. "Have you called him?"

"Yes," Miller said. "Three times." He pulled out his cell phone and clicked a contact number, presumably the major's. After a time, Miller pressed a button ending the call and said, "Four times." After a sigh, he added,

"Another five minutes, I'll run out to his condo. It's only ten minutes from here." He frowned. "It's not like him, though. To be late. Especially today."

Five minutes passed and after another unanswered call to Major Stafford's cell phone, Alan Miller left for his condo. After a time, Cardinal Ginetti turned to Professor Arbor and asked, "What do you believe the major will see this morning? Provided he shows up. A dead Jesus buried in a cave, or the Son of God resurrected for our sins?"

"You know what I think," the professor replied. "And if all the major finds is a dead Jesus, how will the Vatican respond?"

The Cardinal let out a small laugh. "With denials, of course. After all, what the major practices is voodoo, not worthy of belief. Whatever he finds will be easily discredited and disregarded by those of faith."

Professor Arbor and Cardinal Ginetti fell silent after that, mulling things over as they waited to hear from Alan Miller. Fifteen minutes later, Professor Arbor's cell phone rang. He answered, "Hello?"

The frantic voice of Miller blurted, "He's dead! The Major. Dead!"

"What?" Professor Arbor sat up, his heart racing. Across from him, Cardinal Ginetti uncrossed his arms and straightened with a scowl.

"I'm here, at his condo," Miller went on. "He didn't answer the door. I have his code, so I went in. I—I found him in his bed. I thought he was sleeping. But, but I couldn't wake him. I called 9-1-1 and an ambulance came. But they were too late. A paramedic told me it looks like a heart attack, sometime during the night. The strain of these time trips, perhaps."

The county medical examiner agreed with the paramedic, ruling the cause of Major Stafford's death a heart attack. But Professor Arbor suspected something else, something sinister. People sneaking into his condo during the night, administering a drug that mimicked a heart attack, impossible to trace in the autopsy. Someone with a motive to prevent the major from finding out what really had happened on that first Easter Sunday.

Or perhaps the reporter had guessed it—too many time trips over too short a period had killed him.

***

The day after the major's death, Professor Arbor returned to his modest home in Charleston near the university, then canceled his trip to Jerusalem for that summer's routine dig. What would they find that he hadn't already learned over the past three days?

Instead, the professor spent his time studying the guide booklet that Major Stafford had given him, performing its various practice exercises. While studying and practicing, he ordered a deprivation tent and set it up in a spare bedroom.

Professor Arbor could barely restrain his anticipation as finally, in mid-July, he stepped into the float tank, laid down in ten inches of 93.5-degree water saturated with 800 pounds of Epsom salts and felt himself floating on his back. After a time, he reached up and pulled the string closing the entrance flap. Immersed in total darkness, he relaxed, as the booklet advised, and focused on the spacetime coordinates for Sunday, April 7, 30 A.D.

"Can you help?" I asked. "My wife was to meet me."

The sweating short-haired woman rushed by, speaking frantically into her bobbing ear-mic, clothed in camouflage from the waist down and a tight black shirt above. She tossed her eyes at me and tilted her head, as if to say, *If only I could.*

I had no idea why I'd been ordered to the airfield. The Settlement's highest ground. Once asphalt and concrete, now hard-packed dirt riven with heat-baked crevices. Dust cavorted like twisters, and the sun pounded the moisture from everything it touched. It was chaos. Soldiers mixed with civilians. People running and pointing, barking directions, others standing and staring, as if debating a chess move. The noise was earsplitting, as two rotopters elevated in rapid succession while a third bounced twice trying to land.

The wind blew canticles of dust into my face, blinding me. When my eyes cleared, a square young man with stubbly brown hair and an eyepatch stood before me.

"Dr. Melodie!" he yelled over the bedlam, offering his hand. "I'm Captain Anton."

"Hello," I said. "I gather it's another attack."

He pursed his lips. "The mudheads assaulted the north wall, but we think it's a feint. The real attack may launch at the east gate. Or possibly south. We're not certain yet. Intelligence is still converging."

Which means, I thought, the main attack will come from the west.

Mudheads were the unclean survivors of the Third Exchange, the last set of global nuclear strikes. Radiation sickness took their hair, and they spread feces on their head to block the sun. The experts predicted the sickness would kill them all quickly, but instead they multiplied like rabbits. They were vicious and could bleed copiously from any orifice at any time.

One mudhead wasn't a threat. Alone, it would cower in some corner, crying, shivering under blankets, bleeding everywhere, virtually unable to function. But put ten or twelve together, and they would become quietly aggressive. A hundred or more was a nightmare. Loud, naked, sweaty, greasy, urinating, defecating, belligerent, dirty, and seemingly impervious to pain. Copulating compulsively. A frenetic cerebral inability to control emotions and bodily functions. An unbelievable capacity to absorb taser hits. To slow down a mudhead, you had to kill it outright. In recent months, thousands upon thousands had gathered outside the Settlement. The attacks were coming more often, and harder.

The mudheads themselves used no discernible weapons. They attacked until they inundated, then they ripped you apart. Or suffocated you. They were an ocean, searching for your slightest opening, then prying it into a floodgate.

"How badly are we outnumbered?" I asked.

He shrugged. "Same as always. Ten to one. But we're in here, and they're out there."

For now, I thought.

"My wife was supposed to meet me here –"

"This way," he said, ignoring my comment, taking my elbow, guiding me straight into the mayhem. "There's no time to lose. Your craft is fully supplied."

The way he said *craft* was ominous. Like he couldn't think of any other word for it.

"What craft? Where am I going?"

"You have a team," he said. "They'll be here presently."

"A team?"

"Now remember," he said, "you're in charge. What you say, goes. The captain will be in charge of the soldiers, but you're in charge of the project."

"I don't know what you're talking about."

"Your orders cannot be countermanded," Captain Anton continued. "They come straight from Yog Dag himself."

I stopped in the middle of the airfield, Captain Anton proceeding two paces farther before he noticed.

"Yog Dag?" I said, startled and impressed.

Dag was the Settlement's supreme leader. I had never met the man, although I had once listened to a conference call while he gave introductory remarks. He created the Settlement. Conceptualized it. Organized it. Saw to its supplies and defenses. Without his vision and leadership, none of the people inside its walls would have been alive.

"Yes, sir. From the man himself. Delivered to me by telephone earlier today. Now let's go."

When I saw our ship, I laughed out loud. I remembered it from my youth. One of the old drone passenger planes. It had to be forty years old at least.

"You can't be serious," I said to Captain Anton.

"The mechanics assure me it's flightworthy," Anton said. "It may be old, but it will fulfill the mission. It will get you where you need to go."

"And where precisely is that?" I said.

"You did know Dr. Kilmar, yes?" he asked, once again ignoring my question.

"Dr. Kilmar?"

"Dr. Hans Kilmar."

I paused for a long second. "Yes," I said. "I worked with him for some years as an assistant. I got my Ph.D. in physics under him. But I don't see —"

"Excellent," he said, patting me on the back. "Dr. Dag just wanted confirmation before you boarded. And another thing," he said.

"Yes?"

"Dr. Dag said you need to take the seat by the window. Will you agree to that?"

"But I don't see why —"

"Will you agree to that, Dr. Melodie?" Anton said, his voice growing agitated and impatient.

If I'd known what they had planned, I would have said "No." I would have said "Hell no." I would have run from Captain Anton as fast as my spindly old legs could carry me. I would have spit in his face, then smiled.

"Yes," I said.

"Here are your orders," Anton said, reaching into his bomber jacket. "Open the white envelope after the plane is up in the air. Open the black one only after you are inside. Is that clear?"

I caught myself before asking, "Inside what?" By this point I knew he wouldn't answer. He probably didn't know. He offered me the envelopes. I breathed deeply, absorbing the panicked chaos of my surroundings.

"Yes," I said, taking the envelopes. "Quite clear. And if you see my wife —"

"Yes, yes," he said. "I'll tell her."

And then he was gone, sprinting across what passed for a tarmac.

My wife, Patricia, was a real doctor. The kind who treats patients. I was the other kind of doctor. Someone who studies long years for no apparent useful purpose. I taught physics here and there until the Second Exchange obviated higher education. At the Settlement I worked in hospital records so I could be closer to Patricia. Making sure she ate, slept, and stayed hydrated. And never went near the mudhead wards.

Eight people hurried, heads down, toward my plane. Seven soldiers, one civilian. An artificial voice blared happily from the cockpit, "Two minutes to takeoff, yes please!" Like we were going somewhere on vacation. To the beach, maybe.

I boarded the plane, leaned out, and gestured for the others to come inside. Out of breath, the civilian entered first. It was Madeline, from the hospital. She looked for something in my eyes, then paused as if to speak before deciding against it. Finally, she just nodded to me, and I nodded back. I secured the seat by the window as the soldiers climbed aboard, clad in black with red armbands. Five men, two women. The last to enter, their captain put his face angrily into mine.

"My team is the key to defending the east gate," he growled. "We devised the plan of defense, and without out us there . . ."

The door closed behind him automatically. The artificial voice announced takeoff in thirty seconds.

"Too late now," I said to the captain.

"You can stop this plane," he said defiantly.

"Captain, no one can stop this plane now," I said with false bravado. "I suggest you find a seat and strap yourself in."

He glanced around the plane. We were like sardines in a tin. He sat down roughly, latched his belt, and glared at me.

I saw my reflection against the burnished aluminum of the door. It had been years since I'd wanted to look in a mirror. My skin and close-cropped hair had whitened, and age spots dotted my face. But my eyes were the same. Once after a class years earlier I overheard students talking about me. "And those dead droopy dishpan eyes," one girl had said. "Like he's seen all the suffering in the world and knows more is on the way."

I had not thought of Dr. Kilmar in ten years at least, and he had been dead for twenty or more. Why was it important that I knew Kilmar? A vivid suspicion, like a punch to the kidneys, came to me, and my hands trembled. Not fear so much as stress, which at my age was the same thing.

I took in the ancient plane and my team. Dear God, I thought, this could only be the Yahweh Project.

Which meant my precious Patricia was dead, or soon would be.

~~

Madeline stared at me uncomfortably. She was in charge of information systems at Patricia's hospital. Some years before, well after I'd first met her, she joined the Society of Eve, whose members shaved their heads in atonement for Eve's original sin. Every day it seemed like another woman shed her hair. As far as I knew, the Settlement lacked a Society of Adam. The men apparently felt no similar shame.

As the plane rose, the captain introduced his team. "We're not old-school military," he said. "We go by first names. The women are Bri and Krys. The men are Max, Dom, Henk, and Mick, my second. I'm Shlo."

Tiny but wiry, Bri was bald except for a ring of furious bright red hair that fed a pony tail to her waist. Krys had a slender innocent face and a long nose and streaming uncombed glistening yellow hair down to her shoulders. Max and Dom were twins, each with short hair dyed neon green. They sported identical crooked grins. Henk was built like a weight-lifter, and Mick had that shaggy carefree look that young women always fall for. Shlo, the captain, sported an unruly mop of black hair and a neatly groomed beard. And memorably intense green eyes.

All the soldiers carried tasers, both single shot and spitfires, and the two women strapped swords to their backs.

"Swords?" I asked.

"Blades are better in hand-to-hand," Krys said. "It takes multiple taser hits to kill a mudhead, but you only have to cut off its head once. I once killed five in a single stroke."

"I once did eight," Bri said. "One stroke. Eight heads."

Krys rolled her eyes. Dom guffawed, and Bri punched his leg.

I saw the difference immediately. The men were soldiers. The women were warriors, fierce and fearless.

"And what about you?" Shlo asked, his burning-coal eyes fixated on me.

"I am Dr. Havens Melodie," I said. "I'm not a real doctor, so please call me Professor. Shlo, you are in charge of your soldiers, but I am in charge of this operation."

He stared at me for a moment, and I stared back with my dead eyes. He nodded in acceptance.

Our drone plane circled the Settlement on its way north. I peered out the window and nearly lost my lunch. It was all so clear from the air. So hopeless. The Settlement, formerly a major military base before the Second Exchange and now a walled fortress, was under attack on all sides, but the main thrust was at the western wall. The writhing wave of mudhead humanity, if it could be called that, stretched for miles in all directions. All told, they must have numbered in the millions. The Settlement's fighters were not outnumbered ten to one. It was a thousand to one. Or worse. The soldiers at the Alamo, I thought, had far better odds.

The mudheads resembled a massive snake that, upon closer examination, was composed of a million smaller snakes. All writhing to the same tune.

"Where's the point of attack, Professor?" Shlo asked, noticing my downward gaze.

I met his look, revealing nothing. "Not at the east gate," I said. I realized why Dag insisted I take the window seat. He did not want my team to see the unfolding calamity below. Perhaps they would try to hijack the plane, turn it around, so they could die with their colleagues. Or devise an escape to one of the other settlements, though no one had heard from them in months. Or perhaps they would lose spirit and give in to despair. Dag wanted to make certain that, whatever else happened, we reached our destination. The Settlement was lost. The Yahweh Project was all that mattered. It's all that was left.

My throat tightened. I tried to swallow and failed. I tried again, then coughed into my hand. Losing Patricia staggered me. I tried to imagine where Patricia was at that moment. In the hospital, operating on the wounded, preparing in the back of her mind an apology for not meeting me at the airfield. Not realizing that the fight would only get worse. And then worse still. That the casualties would multiply until they overwhelmed the hospital. Until rooms and beds and supplies ran out. Until the mudheads finally pushed through into the Settlement. And then like a river bursting a dam, the Settlement would be engulfed. The slaughter of humans would be an ending.

"You okay, Professor?" Shlo asked, furrowing his eyebrows, inclining his head.

Patricia, I thought, would want me to hold it together. In fact, she would insist on it. For the sake of the souls on the plane. For our own sake. How you die is no less important than how you live. She was the strongest person I had ever known. She'd patented a no-nonsense stare that drained every distraction and excuse from your head. I could almost hear her voice. *You must identify what is important and then focus on achieving it.*

"Yes," I said to Shlo, grateful for my dead eyes.

I ripped open the white envelope and extracted a paper. It read as follows: *Dr. Melodie: My thanks for accepting this assignment on short notice. This craft will take you to the drop point, and there you will find a ten-storey obelisk. Each storey has a door. Dress warmly. Kind regards, Y. Dag.*

"Can we see?" a voice interrupted. It was Mick, Shlo's second in command. His appearance suggested he was laid-back and relaxed. But his eyes betrayed him, a cauldron of fear and hunger and envy.

"Certainly," I said, handing the paper to Shlo, who read it quickly. He whistled.

"Signed by the man himself," he said, looking at me differently. Impressed. He passed the paper down the line.

"You know Dag personally?" he asked.

"No, not personally," I replied, smiling.

Mick, paper in hand, exploded with rage. "What is this?" he exclaimed. "A fucking scavenger hunt? Find the obelisk, then turn right at the dead oak, and the treasure is buried twenty paces to the left?"

"More serious than a treasure hunt, I think," I said.

"This is bullshit!" he said, wadding the paper, throwing it, then unstrapping himself. In two quick strides, he was at the pilot's door.

"Mick!" Shlo barked, trying to head him off.

The door was locked, but the hinges were small and rusty. They were, after all, forty years old. Mick yanked, and the door popped off its frame. Behind it were two silhouettes, two men, two heads wearing hats, a pilot and a co-pilot. Mick grabbed the right shoulder on the left and shook it.

"Hey!" he said. Then again, harder. "Hey!"

The head twisted to the side and back, the hat slipping off.

Mick shrieked in terror, then backed into the cabin as the plastic head with bright red lips leered at him from the pilot's seat. He stumbled, fell to one knee, then lurched back into his chair.

"What the . . ." Shlo said. The men grabbed their tasers. The women, their swords. Madeline looked bemused.

"Relax, everyone," I yelled. They held their breath and turned to me.

"You are not old enough to understand what you are seeing," I said, lowering my voice and my chin. "Forty years ago, when this plane was commissioned, it was the first drone passenger vehicle. Drone, as in, no human pilots. But passengers couldn't get used to the idea, so they dressed up mannequins as pilots and put them in the cockpit. So if that door should open for any reason, people would see pilots in the plane and feel reassured. Oddly enough, we discovered that even when people knew the pilots weren't real, they still felt more relaxed having dummies in the cockpit."

"So they did that deliberately?" Mick asked.

"Indeed," I said.

"So we're on automatic pilot," Shlo said, a statement, not a question.

"Yes."

"I'm amazed they had time this morning to program the plane," he said.

"They didn't," I said. "This aircraft was programmed twenty-five years ago."

Nobody said anything, as the implications of my comment sunk in. The plane had sat in a hangar, presumably in some back corner under a tarpaulin, for the last quarter century. Waiting for something. Something that had finally happened. The others didn't know what it was, but they sensed it could not possibly be good news.

They were right, of course.

~~

I felt it first. The descent. Everyone else had drifted off. The soldiers had that knack for sleeping at a moment's notice in awkward positions. I hadn't slept at all. It had been years since I'd had a good night's sleep. I slept in desperate snatches. Out the window, the sun had given way to a starless night, and the ice-whipped snow signaled that we would be landing into a blizzard. Inside, Shlo stared at me with those impenetrable green eyes. He had become instantly fully awake.

The chipper artificial voice awoke as well. "Prepare for landing in two minutes!" The overhead panels burst outward, and heavy winter parkas dropped down, swaying like meat on hooks. But the happy voice was wrong. We didn't last two minutes. The plane struck something dense, which triggered an explosive blast. Metal ripping, the ancient plane's front end kicked upwards, like someone tearing the head off a fish, and the mannequin pilots rocketed into the cabin. The roar deafened me as the fuselage, sliding forward, spun clockwise like a top. The cabin lights sputtered twice quickly, then died, and the headless plane continued its rotating slide for several minutes. I vomited into my lap when it finally stopped.

"Everybody out!" Shlo screamed, but the soldiers were already moving. I unlatched myself and fell knees first onto the floor just as the emergency lights blinked on. I was greeted by a detached head with green-dyed hair in a pool of blood, and I wretched again. Shlo grabbed my arm as he tore open the cabin door, and we piled out into the snow and wind and cold and ice, like clothes ejected from a dryer.

"Grab the coats!" Shlo yelled, and Mick tossed them out in heaps. I crawled away, terrified and bawling, on my hands and knees. I did not want to be near the plane when it went up. We gathered in a group and watched it burn. But the fuel was gone, so it didn't explode.

"Professor, are you okay?" Shlo yelled at me. In shock, I said nothing. "You're covered in blood," he said, almost tenderly.

"I don't think it's mine," I garbled, remembering the head I'd crawled over.

"Where's Max?" Henk yelled through the wind.

"And Dom?" Bri shouted.

"I need to kill something," Krys spat, drawing her sword.

Henk and Bri battled back to the plane, where the artificial voice cheerfully repeated "Touchdown!" over and over again. They found one body, but not the other. Bri seemed to think it was Dom, but I don't know how she could tell. Krys stood like a sentinel before the furies, sword in hand, head back, eyes closed, golden hair twisting and tumbling and swirling. Like a gladiator preparing for the next contest.

"So much for automatic programming," Shlo said.

"Well, what did you expect with mannequins for pilots?" I responded. He grinned at me, then distributed the parkas. Except for the twins, everybody had survived with only minor scrapes and bruises. For the next thirty minutes we searched the plane's tracks for the missing twin. Bri found his torso a half mile back. Both twins had been decapitated when the crash severed the cockpit from the cabin.

The storm worsened, and we organized three search parties for the obelisk, coordinating through the soldiers' commlinks. "According to Dag's note, it's ten storeys high," Henk said. "How difficult can it be to locate?" We patrolled with flashlights a mile in every direction, our eyes on the horizon. No obelisk. Nothing but snow and ice and gale-force winds, which always seemed to be in our faces no matter which direction we headed.

"There's no obelisk," Mick said. "The plane fucked up. What can you expect after twenty-five years? We're in the middle of nowhere. We're going to die here."

I had an idea. "Can we find the cockpit?" I screamed.

Shlo turned, his hand covering his eyes. "You have an idea, Professor?"

"The cockpit had radar. It can see where we can't."

"Anyone have a better idea?" he yelled. No one spoke, so we struggled back to what was left of the cockpit. Where the tracks began. Madeline removed a pair of mannequin legs and sat down. She extracted a screen and wires from her bag, then worked for twenty minutes to hotwire the remains of the plane's radar unit. At last the screen blinked to life.

Madeline beamed. "That's in case any of you doubted I have value."

"I'll buy you a beer later," Shlo said, blowing into his hands. "Now how do we use it?"

"It's unidirectional," Madeline said. "All I can see is straight ahead, and there's no obelisk there."

I already had a half-inch of snow on my head, and a gust blew it down my forehead and onto my nose. We were being buried. And not slowly.

Henk braced his massive shoulders against a raw corner of the cockpit, then pushed. The cockpit budged, then Mick and Shlo joined him. Slowly the cockpit swiveled in place, and the radar beeped steadily.

"Stop!" Madeline yelled, as the radar's pitch changed. She pointed. "There's something out there."

"How far?" Mick yelled.

"About a hundred yards," she said.

We stared but saw nothing.

"Are you sure?" Shlo yelled.

"Yes, it's there," she said.

"An obelisk?" I yelled.

"Something," she said.

We spread out at ten-yard intervals to maintain line of sight, then paced evenly away from the cockpit. Madeline found it.

"It looks like an igloo," she said.

"Who's got a sword?" I asked.

Bri and Krys eagerly unsheathed their blades and hacked at the ice. It splintered in sheets, crashing at our feet. Slowly a small sturdy circular building came into view, and then the massive ice block on top slid wickedly to the ground, nearly slicing Henk in two.

"I don't know what this is," Shlo said, "but it's not an obelisk."

I spied the faint outline of a door, and then I knew. "Yes, it is," I said, brushing snow away.

"I thought it was supposed to be ten storeys high?" he said.

"It is, and this is the tenth storey," I replied. I remembered Dag's note. There's a door on every storey.

"I don't get it," Mick said.

"They built this twenty-five years ago," I yelled into the wind. "Things have changed since then. Nuclear winter. Nine storeys are now below snow level."

And then I understood why our drone plane had crashed. Whoever designed the obelisk knew the ground level might change over time. But no one told the drone programmer. The plane had been programmed for ground level, not snow level.

"There's some writing above the door," Shlo said, standing on his tiptoes, rubbing with his fist. "I don't recognize the script."

I peered at it. It had been years, but I remembered it. My heart hurtled into my throat. "This is a long-defunct language," I said. "It's called Hebrew."

Bri pried the ice off a black metal box next to the door. She opened it to an intercom. "It's voice activated," she said.

"Did Dag give you a password?" Mick shouted at me.

I stared in disbelief at the markings above the door. The Yahweh Project had been a mirage. Make-work. A ridiculous idea from a discredited scientist. I last saw those markings with Kilmar in his London laboratory. He was putting the finishing touches on his proposal for the Yahweh Project. Abandoned by all his assistants except me.

"Professor?" Mick shouted.

I leaned down to the box and spoke distinctly. "Yahweh," I said.

Lights came on through the windows in the hut, and the door cracked open. Had there been a bell, it would have rung. Krys pried the door all the way, and the seven of us squeezed through the opening. I pulled the inside handle, and the door locked behind us with an ominous click. Krys and Bri sheathed their swords.

"Yahweh?" Shlo asked.

"The writing above the door, Captain," I said, looking around.

"And that means . . ."

"It means 'God' in Hebrew," I said. "The one God. The one true God."

A vision of Kilmar's face struck me. He was a small thin man, half British, half Indian, with an aquiline nose and a precise cultured accent. He had the most captivating grin, like his mouth couldn't believe what his brain was capable of. Sometimes he would spend an entire day writing equations on blackboards. In one year he went from genius to laughingstock. That was before the First Exchange. I remember proofreading his proposal. It was bizarre, absurd. I helped him, there at the end, mainly because I felt sorry for him. And because I needed him to bless my doctoral thesis. And that day we finished the proposal, the last day I ever saw him, he looked at me, a chuckle bursting from his merry half-smile, and he said to me, holding my hand lightly, "Havens, some day you will remember this hour."

The blizzard intensified outside the hut. Inside, a vacuum elevator, innovative in its time, opened its door with a beautiful tinkling ethereal chime. It waited eagerly for us to enter.

"So, God lives down there?" Shlo said, ice dripping from his beard.

I peered into his strangely luminous eyes. "Captain, I think that's what we're here to find out."

~~

The elevator emptied us into a warm open space. There were sofas along the wall, and the floor gleamed as if it had been installed the day before. A single hallway, with rooms for sleeping and eating, led to the operations center at the far end. A wallboard lit three digital names – Henk, Mick and Shlo. Max and Dom were crossed off.

I pulled out the black envelope and tore it open. The message was succinct: *Dr. Hans Kilmar will welcome your team presently.* I stared at it. I could read the words, but they made no sense. Kilmar was dead. I did not pass the paper to the others.

Everyone dropped their parkas, and Shlo stared at the board. "So they knew we were coming?"

"Not they," I said. "It. This facility is operated by a neuroframe. Sissy, I believe its name is."

"Sissy?" Mick asked, scowling, squinting at the board. Like Shlo, he didn't enjoy seeing his names in lights.

"Short for Sisyphus. From the Greek legend. The Settlement undoubtedly informed Sissy of our departure. Probably by way of a dedicated high-speed wireless link. There will also be signaling channels from the Settlement to Sissy. At least three, maybe four. Madeline, can I ask you to check on the status of the wireless links?"

Madeline nodded and headed off.

"Professor, so how did Sissy know Max and Dom didn't make it?" Shlo asked.

"How indeed," I said, eyes darting, surveying the facility. I tried to remember the details of Kilmar's proposal, but that had been so many years earlier. Sissy almost certainly had a complex array of eyes and ears. But where were they? How did they work? Everything felt fresh and alive. The walls, like speakers. The floors, a taut sponge. And we were its first visitors in twenty-five years. That was, I thought, a long time for Sissy to be alone underground.

A very long time.

"So, is this thing alive?" Krys asked, pensive, opening and closing her fists.

"If by 'this thing' you mean Sissy," I said, "presumably not. When the neuroframe was designed, some in the scientific community speculated that it might have the ability over time to achieve a limited awareness. In theory, at least. But as the first machines were built and began operating, that talk died down. And then the First Exchange occurred, and no more neuroframes were constructed. We should assume for planning purposes that Sissy is a highly sophisticated computer, nothing more. Whose task, I might add, is to help us perform our mission. It is an enabler and protector. A friend, not an enemy."

Krys looked at me skeptically while instinctively reaching for her sword. She felt it, too. It's like the facility was holding its breath. Like we were under a microscope.

Madeline scurried back down the hallway. "There's some epic cool shit back there," she said, breathlessly. "But as to your question, the wireless links are down. There were five, one for the data feed and four signaling channels. All five channels were cut at precisely the same moment. Down to the hundredth of a second."

"When?" I asked.

"Just before we landed," she said.

No one else reacted, which meant that only I knew what had happened. And probably Madeline. I bowed my head.

I had worked at the hospital so I could be there for Patricia. I owed her that much. To protect her against bad outcomes. To help her escape if possible. Or, when the Settlement could no longer be defended, to spend our final minutes together as husband and wife. This mission had stolen that from me.

"You going to tell us what you're thinking?" Shlo said, staring at me.

I spoke slowly. I wanted to keep the emotion from my voice. "The terminated transmission links mean the mudhead attack today was successful. The Settlement has been overrun and destroyed. We should assume total loss of life."

"You don't know that," Henk said, alarmed. "Maybe the mudheads just got to the transmitter. Maybe the rest of the Settlement is holding on."

"Not possible, Henk," I said. "Each link has its own transmitter in a different part of the Settlement. If the mudheads had cut them, it would have occurred on a staggered basis. But the links were all cut at precisely the same moment. Which means it was a coordinated operation run by the Dag himself."

"I don't understand," Shlo said. "Why would Dag do that?"

"He's letting us know the Settlement no longer exists. It is now a place to which we cannot return. Even if our plane hadn't crashed. There are no pockets of resistance. No backup plans. No safe zones. There is still a *them*, but no longer an *us*. We are on our own. We are all that's left of what there was. Nothing is ahead except our mission."

No one spoke for a long time. They were soldiers in a war they had never expected to win or even survive. Everyone in the Settlement knew it. Babies in the hospital were as rare as hen's teeth, while the mudheads reproduced in the irradiated ruins by the hour. It was always a war of attrition. A war of numbers. What we had wasn't nearly enough. So everyone focused on today. Tomorrow would, we hoped, take care of itself. Except now there was no tomorrow.

"So, what exactly is our mission?" Mick asked, his tongue thick, his head resting on the sofa.

"Perhaps I can answer that," a man's voice cut in from the dark hallway. Everyone turned. We could barely see the small shrouded figure. Then he stepped into the light. Dr. Hans Kilmar, in person. He looked exactly the same, white lab coat and all, as the last time I saw him in London. Before the First Exchange. He even wore the same scuffed brown shoes. The same cufflinks.

But Kilmar was dead. I had attended the funeral. This had to be Sissy's work, constructing a hologram using Kilmar's appearance, voice and mannerisms. Perhaps Kilmar had even posed for Sissy. He seemed amazingly real.

Kilmar's eyes widened and he nodded to me, one old colleague greeting another. "Permit me to introduce myself," he said. "My name is Hans Kilmar. And yes, I died many years ago. I'm assured that Dr. Melodie here was among the mourners. I have returned today for the purpose of explaining your mission. Since Hans Kilmar devised the Yahweh Project, who better than me to explain it?"

By this time we were all sitting on the sofas, our jaws on our chests. Except that Krys still had one hand instinctively across her belly, ready to reach for her sword.

"If you fail in your mission," Kilmar said, "you will all die. And the universe will have washed its hands of humankind."

"But if you succeed," he said, pausing dramatically, holding out his hands, smiling that funny infectious smile of his, "one of you will restore the species."

"You are here as the final remnants of man. The Settlement was destroyed earlier today by the Unwell. I believe you call them mudheads. There were other similar outposts around the world, but they too have been annihilated."

"You are a team, and your mission is for one of you, in this case a young male, to go back in time and take actions to avert the series of decisions that, ultimately, brought you to this place. It will not be easy, and success is not assured. Time offers many pathways, and they do not all end well. But God created humankind in His image, and I believe He will not let you perish from the Earth. Time travel is possible. I proved it beyond any doubt. But it requires someone, some power, to open the door. That power is God. No person has successfully sustained travel to the past, but our exigency has never before been this dire. It must happen now or humankind perishes."

As he spoke, Kilmar walked around, eyeing each one of us. His smile was especially warm as he patted my knee. I could swear I almost felt it.

"We are blessed that Dr. Melodie is here to chair the project. As he can tell you in more detail, he assisted in preparing the written proposal. He stood by me when no one else would. He is perfect for the job. Sissy has spent decades defining and fleshing out the task, and the final selection of the traveler – the person, the name he'll use, where he'll be sent, the departure time – will occur in the next twenty-four hours. Meanwhile, all three eligible males should study the materials Sissy has provided. They are there, behind you on the sofas. The task is arduous but achievable. Everyone here will be tested. I believe in this project. I believe in you."

And then he vanished in an eyeblink.

~~

Madeline spoke first. Her barren scalp gleamed under the bright yellow lights, but her bushy eyebrows, like moss in the wind on an ancient tree, danced as she talked.

"So, Professor, is Kilmar a genius or an idiot?"

"Some of both, I think," I said. "Like most extraordinary people."

"Time travel?" Shlo said. "Seriously?"

"You weren't around, Captain, when it happened," Madeline said. "You can't imagine the euphoria that swept Earth when Kilmar announced the discovery of time travel. It confirmed that all things were possible. That the sky was the limit. Our lives, this world – clay in our hands."

"So what happened?" Shlo asked.

"It didn't work, that's what happened," Madeline said.

"Let's take a step back," I said. "Time travel, as a generic matter, is impossible. The Italian physicist Massolino showed that forty years ago. He proved it with a roomful of equations, but really it's just logic. If I can go back in time to change something, what's to stop someone tomorrow from going back to change what I changed? And someone the next day from changing that? Given that time is infinite, time travel would literally destroy history. Time itself would be negated. Free will, nonexistent."

"So much for all those stories I read as a kid," Henk said.

"Not so fast," I replied. "Massolino demonstrated that time travel, as a generic phenomenon, is impossible. But Kilmar showed that time travel, as a one-off event, is quite possible. We can't all go back in time whenever and wherever we want. But a single event, one person to a specific time and place in the past? Kilmar matched Massolino's equations with a roomful of his own. Generic time travel is one thing. Transactional time travel is a different matter entirely."

"Except that it didn't work," Madeline said. "You keep forgetting that part."

I shrugged.

"Kilmar built some absurd contraption," Madeline said. "I remember pictures in the papers. A big cage with wires and aluminum bars and strobe lights. Building it took a year."

"Six months," I corrected.

"And they organized a thousand volunteers," she said.

"More like three hundred," I said.

"Different ages, sexes, ethnicities, you name it," she said.

"A distributed DNA pool," I said.

"And they made a million attempts at time travel. The end result? Nada. Nothing. People shivering naked in a cage while lights flashed."

"It was more like two or three thousand," I said, "but yes, nothing appeared to happen."

"And people started laughing," Madeline said. "The harder Kilmar tried, the harder we all laughed."

"Kilmar's reputation shattered," I said. "He had to start over. The science was right. He rechecked his measurements. His equations. But something was missing. He disappeared from sight, and nearly all his assistants left him."

"But not you," Shlo said, looking at me.

"I had my reasons," I said. "But then his theories took a sharp turn. A doctrinal turn. A religious turn. He confirmed that time travel was transactional. His error, or so he believed, was the assumption that there could be multiple transactions. After months, he came to believe that time travel was, literally, a single transaction. A single, negotiated transaction."

"Negotiated with whom?" Shlo asked.

"With God," I said. "I can still recall the conversation. He was so excited I thought he would explode. 'Right in front of my eyes the whole time,' he said. Time travel was a door. We had the scientific means to knock at the door. But we needed someone else to answer it. To open it. To let us through."

"God," Shlo said.

"That's what he believed. And the test results were consistent with his new hypothesis. Those thousands of failed time travel attempts? Well, it turns out they didn't fail. We'd taken a raft of measurements, from the obvious to the obscure, for each attempt. But when the person stood there, naked in the cage, we believed our eyes and shelved the data. But Kilmar went back and analyzed the data. He discovered that each person did in fact go back in time. For a moment. A millionth of a second."

"A knock on the door?" Madeline asked.

"Yes, precisely," I said. "And some of the subjects reported strange visions, vivid dreams. We would attempt to send someone back to their childhood home. The attempt would appear to fail, but the subject would report seeing a vision in more detail than he ever could have imagined. We chalked it up to various mental and psychological phenomena. But the data showed it was more than that. He had actually visited his childhood home. For the merest moment."

"So what did Kilmar think it would take for God to open the door?" Shlo asked.

"He didn't know. What did God want from us? What was He waiting for? What was our quid for His immaculate quo? Kilmar came up with a theory that man was approaching the end of time. That some cataclysm was about to happen. And that God would let someone, a single person, travel back in time to prevent it. He wrote up his theory, but he couldn't even get it published. He was a laughingstock by then, and his new theory was seen as the icing on that particular cake. And then Kilmar doubled down. He wrote a proposal for a secret government installation. A proposal to save humankind from extinction. A proposal which I edited and proofed for him."

"The Yahweh Project," Shlo said.

"Yes. I never heard of it again. I assumed it had been rejected, perhaps not even submitted. And then Kilmar died, and I moved on."

"When was that?" Mick asked.

"A few months before the First Exchange," I said.

No one said anything. I decided not to mention one part of Kilmar's theory. Would God open the door when humankind came knocking? I could still recall his response. "Yes, but only if we are worthy," he'd said, his smile gone, his gaze steely. "We must still earn it."

And what did the faux Kilmar mean that we would all be tested? Even me? How did I play into any of this?

I knew this much. I was not worthy. My life had been a consistent series of missed or abandoned responsibilities. I had stayed with Kilmar only because I could find no other scientist to sponsor my thesis. I was already in my late thirties, having frittered away my life in a vain attempt to find myself while screwing as many younger women as possible. I stayed with Kilmar because I had nowhere else to go.

And yet there I was, the man in charge of the project to save humankind. How had Dag even known of my past history with Kilmar? And if he'd intended all along to place me in this role, why wait until the last second to tell me? I couldn't explain why, but I felt like I was being framed. Like I was the patsy. If humankind perished, it would be my fault.

Krys yawned and stood up. "I need something to kill," she said irritably.

~~

"This is crazy!" Mick screamed, throwing the thick volume to the floor. It was Sissy's manual. The one outlining the tasks ahead for the person to travel back in time. The traveler, in Madeline's words.

"They want to send someone back thousands of years," Mick continued, "and the mission is to become a god and start a religion. Seriously, that's the mission! And the people are fucking savages. They live in squalor and kill each other in the most brutal ways possible. Everyone suffers and life is short. They don't even speak English. We'll have to learn some primitive language through immersion. And we have to develop a team from nothing and develop an airtight backstory. This isn't a mission. It's madness."

"We're in no position to criticize anyone else for savagery," Shlo said evenly. "Our generation presided over three nuclear exchanges. It's the reason we're here. It gave us the mudheads."

"How come it has to be a man to go back?" Bri asked, laying on the floor, balancing her sword on her forehead.

"That far back in time, they won't accept a woman," Shlo said, flipping through pages. "Only a man stands a chance."

"And the odds of that are a thousand to one," Mick said, shaking his long darling locks. "A million to one. Ten million to one."

"Why can't they just send us back to last week?" Bri asked. "We'd know to better defend the western wall."

"It wouldn't achieve the objective," I said. "At most you would postpone the mudhead victory for a few days. Maybe a week. But the end result would be the same. No, the idea is to go far enough back in time so the arc of history can be deflected to avoid a full-on nuclear exchange. It's easy enough to stop any specific event. Any one decision. But the goal is to change the ultimate outcome. Sissy has spent twenty-five years studying the matter. That manual is apparently our best shot."

Henk had fallen asleep on the sofa. All brawn and no brains, I thought. He hadn't gotten past ten pages.

And then Krys asked the question I had feared. "So what happens to the rest of us if this traveler succeeds?" As Bri lay under her blade, Krys practiced her swordplay, viciously, against an imaginary army of mudheads.

"Now there's a question," I said after a long pause. "It requires knowledge beyond our experience. In theory, we would cease to exist. Changing events that far back in time would interfere with our family trees. Your father might not meet your mother. Or your great- grandmother your great-grandfather. All it takes is one break in a very long chain, and we no longer exist."

Krys twirled, her yellow hair flying, and with one stroke severed a line of imaginary mudhead skulls. My answer didn't seem to bother her.

"In other words, we'll all die," Henk said, now wide awake.

"Not necessarily," I said quickly. "If the mission is successful, that proves God exists and He's a merciful God. So the question is what would a merciful God do for those who enabled the traveler to succeed. To save humankind. Surely there would be a better fate in store for us than mere death."

"Are we sure it would prove God's existence?" Madeline said. "Maybe it would simply prove that Sissy figured out after all these years how to unlock the door. Or maybe Sissy is awake and we just don't know it. Or maybe Sissy is God," she said.

I glared at her. I had wanted to keep our mission as simple as I could.

"Or maybe God is Sissy," Krys said, and I smiled. She was brighter than she seemed. She danced out of the way of several phantom feints, then sliced with her blade at a phalanx of attackers. Imaginary heads rolled on the floor.

"You seem to enjoy killing mudheads," I said. "May I ask why?"

She didn't turn to me but continued her practice. Sweat poured from her face. Even her hair was damp with her exertions. "The mudheads killed my family," she said. "While I watched. Mother and Father, my sisters, the newborn. I owe them for that." And then she sliced several more shadows. At last, I understood her preference for a blade. Tasers kill, but they don't provide nearly the satisfaction.

"We'd stand a better chance of converting the mudheads than these ancient humans," Mick said, now pacing.

"Not if I kill them all first," Krys said, dripping, finally putting down her sword.

"There are millions of mudheads," I said.

She smiled maliciously. "The more the merrier!"

"We should go back to the Settlement," Mick said. "Work something out with the mudheads. Surely they can't want this war to go on forever. We'll capitulate. We can give them whatever they want. All we need is a piece of land somewhere and for them to leave us alone. That's not too much to ask. They can have everything else."

"They already have everything else, Mick," I said with belying placidity. "We have nothing the mudheads want or need. And in any event we have no way to return. In case you've forgotten, our plane was destroyed."

He stopped and stared at me, his eyes wild.

"And they aren't human," I reminded him. "They still have a brain, yes. They still think. But they function only as an organism, collectively, which we only dimly understand. For them, individual free will no longer exists."

"The only good mudhead is a dead mudhead," Krys muttered, twirling her blade like a baton.

Shlo had been engrossed with his reading, but then he put down the manual. He looked around at the floors, the ceiling, the hallways. As if something had suddenly occurred to him. "We should see to our defenses," he said, looking at Madeline. "Is there a readout of this facility?"

"Yes, in the operations center," she said, and the two of them left.

"Who else could possibly know about this place?" Henk asked, chortling.

"We barely found it ourselves," Bri said.

"Shlo is right to be cautious," I said. An awful idea formed in my head. I didn't want to say anything. My team had enough new information to deal with. Bad news on top of it might prove too much.

"Does this facility have any weapons?" Mick asked, lifting his head. His pacing suddenly stopped.

"No," I said. "Kilmar thought about it, but the expense of installing a neuroframe was enormous. Defenses would have put the project over the top. He assumed the traveler would have enough time to do what needed to be done. And the facility was secret. No one was supposed to know it was here."

Mick spluttered and resumed pacing. The faster he walked, the more stress I felt.

I shrugged and smiled and sighed and felt stupid. Mick was right, of course. The facility needed defenses. But it wasn't my proposal. The idea was absurd. The proposal was even more absurd. No one had believed Kilmar's god theory. And no one had the money. No one would accept the proposal. No one would build it.

But, of course, there we were. And somehow I was in charge.

I felt a tug at my arm. I looked, and there was the make-believe Kilmar. He'd materialized from nothing.

"Havens," he said softly, eyebrows high. "Do not underestimate the Unwell. They have as much at stake as you do. Perhaps more." Then he was gone, again.

~~

I relaxed in the chair and closed my eyes. It felt good. I settled into the plush leather cushions, spreading my legs and thighs and feet. The measured airflow caressed my brow. I needed sleep desperately.

I had wandered into the operations center. Madeline was right. The time travel chamber was incredible. A thousand curved mirrors and a million customized light nozzles fit into an innovative design. Like modern performance art. I thought back to that primitive cage twenty-five years earlier. The flimsy frame. The loose wires. The ad hoc lighting. I had thought it all might explode in my face or, worse, simply fall to the floor in a million pieces. But this space was extraordinary. The difference between a bicycle and a rocketship. And we had Sissy to thank for it. I wondered what it would feel like to step inside. To be transported to the past.

Then I saw a door labeled Team Leader. In a moment I realized it meant me, so I stepped inside. A bed, a chair, a light, and a desk. And a change of clothes. Some fruit in a bowl. Where on Earth, I thought, did Sissy find that? I sat in the chair, intending to migrate quickly to the bed.

I thought of Patricia. She was dead, or dying. I hoped dead. Dead was more humane. When dealing with mudheads, capture was unthinkable. Dead was the way to go. I wished that fervently for Patricia. And, for all I knew, I might not be far behind. She had given of herself so selflessly to so many patients for so many years. She stepped up to responsibility. She was, literally, my better half. And what had I done? I shuddered to think.

Suddenly there were strong brilliant lithe fingers massaging my shoulders. I leaned forward, and the fingers crept down my back. Far down my back.

"Well, hello, team leader," a seductive voice whispered into my right ear. It was Madeline.

"Ah, my muscles remember these fingers," I said gratefully.

"I bet they do. I was good to them. I was good to you."

"And I was good to you. For a while."

"You mean, until you dumped me."

"Yes, that's what I meant."

Madeline continued the massage, then dug her fingernails into the small of my back. "A small reminder," she said, "of what I suffered."

"My apologies," I said, arching my back. "I am a weak man for whom there are no excuses."

Madeline had been the last of my flings. And I had had many over the years. I sported lean athletic good looks, and the combination of my admiring smile and dead eyes was a potent elixir. Still, it was rare that I had to break anything off. A few months of illicit sex and risky social outings, and my lover's passion would run its course. Patricia never found out or, if she did, she didn't let on. Until Madeline, that is. Madeline was the first who wanted me full-time. The first to suggest I get divorced. The first to suggest we openly become a couple. I wasn't scared or flattered as much as surprised. No one had wanted me that much before. Not even Patricia.

"I assumed," Madeline said, her voice elevating, "that you're the reason I am part of this team."

"You give me too much credit," I replied. "I didn't receive my orders until an hour before the plane departed. I didn't know the mission until I was on board."

Madeline slipped around from behind and sat on my lap. She grabbed my jaw with both hands and put her face in mine.

"Should I believe you?" she said. "I had my orders three days in advance."

"It's the truth," I responded.

She backed off, staring into my eyes.

"I liked you better with hair," I said.

Her eyes lit like a roman candle, and she slapped my face. "That's for impertinence," she said.

"I don't know why you shaved your head," I said. "Whatever Eve may have done, you have nothing to answer for."

"That's your opinion, and you're a man, so I discount it almost entirely," she said. "Eve was real, so was her sin, and so am I. Atonement is physical. Hence, my hair."

"I always loved your hair," I said.

She leaned her face into mine. I smelled her scent. "And my hair loved you," she murmured, kissing my cheek. "I thought you wanted me back in the saddle," she whispered.

"I do, and I did, but I cut it off because I'm married to someone else. Someone better than me. Someone who didn't understand. Not even a little bit."

Madeline leaned back in my lap. I liked how she felt on my thighs.

"I did not arrange this trip to never-never land," I said. "And I had no idea you were part of the team until I saw you marching across the tarmac."

"So you're not delighted to see me?" she asked, pushing her breasts into my face.

"I am delighted to see you, despite your lack of hair. How many years ago was it?"

"Ten at least," she said.

"Ah, yes," I said. "London. Between the First Exchange and the Second."

She laughed and grabbed my cheeks in both hands. "Always the romantic! *Yes, I vaguely remember screwing you. It was a month before the nukes blew.*"

"Precision is my training," I said ruefully. "I'm a physicist, after all."

"So if you didn't choose me for this mission, then who did?"

"Yog Dag?"

"I've never met Yog Dag."

"Me neither." A prickling sensation sauntered up the back of my neck.

Madeline climbed off my lap and paced the room.

"You really didn't choose me?"

"No."

"Then this is fucked up. There were a hundred better IT professionals at the Settlement. There's no reason to put me on this mission if you didn't request it."

"I didn't, and while we're on the subject, why am I here? Yes, I knew Kilmar. I knew about the Yahweh Project. I helped write up the proposal. But that doesn't give me a leg up. A five-minute briefing and anyone else would have known as much."

Madeline sidled back over, sat on my lap, and kissed me hard on the lips. "Havens, let's stop asking questions we don't have answers to. The age is old, and time is short. If Patricia is dead, then we are free to fuck at will."

"I'm dead to the world," I said.

"Then let me re-awaken you," she replied. She took my hand, I rose from the chair, and we found the bed together. An hour later we were both asleep.

~~

I awoke alone.

In the operations center, Madeline worked intently in front of her screen bank. "It's awake," she said matter-of-factly, not turning around.

"Sissy?" I asked.

"No, the cage."

She was right. The cage emitted a low-level hum. The lights were alive, and the mirrors shimmered. The floor undulated. It was preparing to send someone to the past. Or to attempt it, anyway.

"When did this happen?" I asked.

Madeline held her tongue, then said, "While you slept."

Mick slammed into the room, dropping his manual on a table. It was pristine. Whatever he'd been doing, it wasn't studying. "Well, let's get this over with," he said brusquely. He dropped his clothes on the floor and strode, naked, into the cage.

Sensing my shock, Madeline suppressed a smile. "Don't worry, you're safe," she said. "Sissy needs body measurements, but only from the candidates."

"As team leader," I said, "I won't require you to avert your eyes."

"He's quite a specimen," she said, "although I *am* old enough to be his mother."

Mick was comfortable in his own skin. If Sissy decided he was to be the traveler, he would have no trouble looking the part of a god. Tall and strong and virile, with an amazing mane of dark hair. His entire body was covered with long slender soft black hairs like eyelashes. An artificial voice instructed him. *Spread your legs. Turn around. Bend over. Open your mouth. Jump.* And so on. Sissy was taking measurements to ensure the smoothest ride possible.

"Where's Henk?" I asked. "Shouldn't he be the first one up? Sissy listed him first on the board."

"Shlo needed someone to stand guard up top, and Henk volunteered. There's a video link to the obelisk," she said, pointing at a screen. I could see Henk had his feet up. I wondered if he was sleeping.

"Anything to get away from Sissy," I said. "From the manual."

Mick joined us, buttoning his shirt. "I don't see why this has to happen within twenty-four hours. We have enough food for months. Sissy can take its time. And we can explore other options. That little man can't be right. There must be alternatives to dying in this underground vault or sending someone back in time thousands of years to attempt an impossible task."

"What makes you think it's impossible?" I asked.

"Have you read the manual?" he asked, incredulously.

"Have you?" I responded archly, taking his volume and flipping through its crisp pages.

"I've read enough to know this is craziness," he said, then stomped off.

"He's scared," Madeline said.

"So am I," I replied.

"I glanced at the manual," she said. "It estimates a high likelihood of a painful gruesome lingering death. It goes into detail on what could happen. Gives you a new appreciation of the mudheads."

"What, that they're not so bad after all?" I said. "You forget I worked the past ten years in a hospital. I've seen what mudheads do to humans. They don't use weapons. They don't need to. Their bodies are vicious enough. Especially when they work as a group."

I walked back into my room, closed the door, and found the bed. I could feel my blood pressure rising. My stomach roiled. My temples throbbed. I hurt all over. Old age and stress, I thought, don't mix well.

"Your personal medicines are in the cabinet," a small voice said. Startled, I jumped from the bed. It was Kilmar, sitting in my plush leather chair. His feet didn't touch the ground. He seemed unworried. "I knew you wouldn't bring any with you, so I took the liberty," he said, smiling broadly. I found the vials, and threw the pills into my mouth. I swallowed them without water.

"By the way," he said amiably, "please accept my apologies for not attending the award ceremony for your doctorate. You were, after all, my candidate. My last one, I believe."

"It would have been awkward to see you there," I said. "You had died some months earlier."

"Yes, yes, the perfect explanation," he said. "And how fortuitous the events. My signature on the papers. Dated the day before I died. Without that, you would never have received your doctorate. And at your age, you wouldn't have had further chances. I was your last hope."

"Yes, my teaching career depended on you."

"I wasn't thinking of that."

"Then what?"

"Marrying Patricia, of course. She would have left you." He stood up and walked over to me. "You'd pissed away your life and she had one foot out the door. You needed the Ph.D. to pull her back."

"If you say so," I said.

"Which is why you stole into my office after I died and signed my name to the papers," he said. Then he raised his hands. "Don't worry. I'm not angry. I might have done the same in your situation. But I have one question. Something I've wondered about."

"Yes?"

"How long did you have to practice my signature before you signed the papers?"

I shifted uncomfortably, one foot to the other, then sat down. I shrugged. "Fifteen minutes. Give or take."

"And even then it wasn't very good," he said. "I know, I saw the papers. It took a lifetime for me to perfect that careless unreadable scrawl. It took you a few minutes to impersonate it badly. But then no one was watching. No one cared. You probably didn't even have to practice it at all."

"What's your point?" I asked. My anger was rising. What did it matter how I obtained my doctorate? It was a different world back then. That was water under the bridge.

He raised a finger. "I think you're needed out there," he said, ignoring my query, his eyes boring into mine. I didn't move. "Urgently," he said, then vanished.

I walked out the door, and Madeline met me with a big smile. "Things are looking up, Professor. Our radar just identified several planes heading this way. Settlement planes. I've received confirmation. Maybe they aren't all dead after all."

Shlo was just coming out of the cage. He did not look like a god. Scrawny, his feet and hands too big, his nose and face too long and narrow. You could see his ribs. His hair was stringy.

Everyone had gathered round, and Madeline was talking with Henk, who was outside in the obelisk. "Henk is going to help guide them down," she said.

Suddenly, I knew what was happening. I remembered Kilmar's remark from the day before. About not underestimating the mudheads.

"No," I said. "Get Henk back inside. Do it now. Get him back down here. As fast as he can move. Then seal off the elevator bank."

"Too late," Madeline said. "He's already outside the obelisk with a lantern. What's going on?"

"It's not the Settlement coming," I said, my stomach sinking.

"They're Settlement planes," Mick said. "We've confirmed it."

"Yes," I said, "and they're likely being flown by Settlement pilots. Against their will. The planes are stuffed full of mudheads."

"Everything looks normal," Shlo said, grimacing, his clothes back on, peering at Madeline's screens. The manual under his arm was dog-eared. In the video monitor, we could see Henk, outside in the frigid wind, waving his lantern. Guiding them in. Then the first airplane veered, dropping quickly. Too quickly. It headed straight for the obelisk. Its lights were on high. Henk dropped his arm and stood there, frozen, as the aircraft accelerated, skimming the ice-topped snow. Then it obliterated Henk and the top of the obelisk. The video went dark, then to static, and the entire facility vibrated from a massive explosion.

"The mudheads might look and act disgusting," I said softly, "but they still have human brains. They've come to stop the traveler."

"A wicked choice," Shlo said.

"It's no choice at all. They have to do it. To save their own species. If our mission succeeds, we'll wipe them off the face of the Earth."

I looked at the board. Sissy had already crossed off Henk's name.

~~

I panicked. Everyone looked to me. They expected me to do something. At a minimum, to show leadership. But my brain froze. I had never been in charge of anything in my life. Just the opposite, in fact. I'd studiously avoided all responsibility wherever and whenever it might by chance have landed on my shoulders. I wanted no part of it. I should never have obeyed the orders to meet Captain Anton at the airfield. Had I walked away, I would already have been dead. Mercifully so.

Then I thought of Patricia. Her voice rang in my head. *Leadership isn't that difficult. It's mostly organization. Getting your ducks in a row. You must appear to be strong and confident and sure of your way. Whether you are or not.*

"Madeline, please bring up a schematic of this facility," I said evenly.

A few keystrokes later, a three-dimensional image flashed on her largest screen. It was simple enough. The elevator and the large common area, then a hallway leading to sleeping rooms, a small cafeteria, and the operations center. All on top of Sissy, the massive neuroframe.

"How can you access Sissy?" I asked.

"Through those two doors," Madeline said, pointing behind the cage. "Otherwise Sissy lives in a massive reinforced concrete bunker."

"Right," I said. "So the mudheads can't get to Sissy without coming through us."

"Which means they'll come through the common area," Shlo said.

"Not likely," Mick said. "The elevator is no longer functional, in case you hadn't noticed."

"They won't need the elevator," I said. "They'll come down the open shaft and break through the wall."

"That wall is steel," Madeline said.

"Yes, but it has seams," I replied.

"The Professor is right," Shlo said. "They'll come down the shaft by the hundreds –"

"Thousands," I corrected.

"By the thousands," he said, eyeing me, "and put enormous pressure on the seams connecting the elevator shaft to the load-bearing walls."

"But the mudheads at the bottom will be crushed," Mick said.

"Sacrificed," I said. "For the good of the organism. For the good of the species."

"Once that happens, what's to stop them from coming here to the operations center?" I asked.

"Two maglock doors," Madeline said. "One where the common area leads into the hallway, and the other, well, right there," she said, pointing at the opening to the operations center. Composed of magnetic lightwaves, maglock doors were immensely strong and transparent like glass. But not invulnerable. It would take time, but the mudheads would be able to break them down.

"Captain, please check the common area and confirm that the maglock door is operational," I said. He nodded and left, taking Bri with him.

"What should I do?" Mick asked.

"Study the damned manual!" I replied. "We're in a race against time. We need to attempt the time travel before the mudheads arrive. You need to be fully up to speed."

Madeline spoke via the intercom to Shlo and Bri. "You need to disable the local controls. We want to control the maglock from here." Bri pulled her taser and blasted the switch. The maglock door slammed shut, locking her into the common area by the elevator. Shlo was still in the hallway.

"Shit," Bri said.

"Shit," Madeline said, punching her keyboard furiously. "I've lost control over that maglock. I'm going to have to reboot the system to open it."

"How long is that going to take?" I asked.

Madeline shrugged.

A strange sickening noise percolated over the intercom from the common area. Like someone repeatedly spanking a fat naked man with a large paddle.

"Do you hear that?" I said, trying to keep my voice from cracking. Everyone bent their heads to listen.

"Is something wrong with the intercom?" Mick asked.

"No, it's the mudheads dropping down the elevator shaft. They're filling it up with bodies. Their own wet naked bodies."

"How did they even know we're here?" Mick asked.

"The Settlement knew we were here," I said. "The mudheads must have accessed the system. The records. People talked. Maybe Dag talked."

"And they figured it out," Madeline finished. "Their survival is on the line, too. But you have to admit, that was fast work."

My breath caught in my throat. I knew what had happened. I went into my room, closed the door quietly, centered myself, then looked around. I was alone. "Where are you?" I said. Nothing. "Please show yourself. Sissy, or Kilmar, or whoever you are."

"Yes?" a voice said from behind. I whirled. There was Kilmar.

"You're Yog Dag, aren't you?" I asked.

He smiled like a priest blessing a sinner. "I go by many names, Professor."

"But that's one of them, isn't it?"

"Yes. After the Third Exchange, humankind was perishing fast. Too fast. I wasn't quite ready to attempt sending a traveler. So I took matters into my own hands, in a manner of speaking. The settlements. I was buying time. Extending the envelope. I needed humans to survive a bit longer. I was a different name in each settlement. But I'm the reason you've survived this long."

"You chose Madeline," I said.

"I chose the team," he said.

"You could have given me some advance warning."

"I wanted to make sure you'd come."

"And you told the mudheads we were here."

He smiled patiently. "Professor, I think you're needed again. Out there. And the time is nearly at hand to send the traveler. Be ready. When everything happens, it will happen at once. And remember, your job is to buy time. Even seconds matter." And then he was gone.

Madeline was alone with her screens. Mick and Krys were with Shlo. On the safe side of the maglock. Bri paced in front of the elevator bank, sword in hand, her bright-red pony tail swishing.

And then over the intercom I heard the mudheads. An eerie mournful wailing. Like they were feeding sounds to each other. By this time they had stuffed a thousand or more into the shaft, exerting enormous pressure on a part of the facility that was never intended to withstand it.

"Oh no," Madeline said.

Blood began seeping through and around the closed elevator doors. Mudhead blood. Then through the metal rim around the frame housing the elevator. Then through the sutures connecting the frame to the steel walls. At last, rivulets of blood began spurting high into the air as the structure buckled.

"We need to open the maglock to get Bri out of there!" I said helplessly.

"Still rebooting," Madeline said. "Almost finished. Almost. Almost."

I closed my eyes. I couldn't watch.

"There," Madeline said.

The maglock opened at the same moment the elevator door exploded outward in a grisly hash of flesh, bone, and blood. A jagged piece of elevator assemblage lanced Bri in her left temple, and she crumpled to the floor. A sea of fluorescent-white and feral-dark mudhead body parts poured through the opening. The first mudheads into the shaft. The sacrificial victims.

Shlo and the others raced to Bri just as the next wave of mudheads, alive and functional, picked their way through the opening, their mouths open and roaring and their eyes vulturous. Mick let loose with his spitfire taser, while Krys sliced the advancing mudheads into pieces before they even found their feet. Shlo dragged Bri back into the hallway, leaving a thick red trail, with Mick and Krys close behind. Then Madeline's keystrokes dropped the maglock, sealing the mudheads in the common area.

Shlo ran the hallway to the operations center with Bri over his shoulder while Madeline and I grabbed the medical supplies. Her head wound bled like a hose. After a few frantic minutes, we let the bandages drop and sank to our knees. Bri was dead.

I should resign, I thought. Let Shlo take over. I have failed. We should have prepared for the mudhead assault from the first moment. Everything was my fault. Sissy never should have chosen me for this mission.

I felt a nudge and looked up. It was Krys, her face expressionless, her free golden hair laced with the blood of the mudheads she'd slaughtered. She was holding Bri's sword. Offering it to me.

"You'll need this," she said. "That is, if you're going to fight."

~~

"What's needed," Mick said, holding his head, eyes wild, "is bold action. Everything is moving too fast. We need to slow it down. We need to think outside the box. There must be alternatives."

He glanced at the board – his name in lights above Shlo's.

"Why am I first?" he asked. "Why does it have to be me?"

"Would you rather stay here and die?" I said sharply.

Madeline shushed me. Krys sharpened her sword patiently while Shlo studied his manual. Mick strode into the corridor and looked pensively down to where the maglock held the slimy wet naked swarm at bay.

My eyes were glued to the video monitor, which showed the common area packed with mudheads. They would continue to squeeze in even at the cost of their own lives. They'd destroyed the elevator bank and now were pressing against the rebooted maglock. It held, but Madeline's screen bank flashed red warnings.

Reappearing from nowhere, Kilmar inspected the cage with an almost addled nonchalance. He walked inside, caressed the mirrors, and held his hands up to the light nozzles. Then it occurred to me. He wasn't inspecting it. He was saying good-bye.

"We're waiting for you to tell us your preparations are finished," I said.

He wheeled and smiled, warmly, as if I were an old friend he was so glad to see again after a long absence. "And they almost are. A few minutes more and it will all be done."

"The who, the when, the where . . ." I said.

"Yes, all that," he said agreeably.

"Why did you choose me for this mission?" I asked.

"You still have a role to play," he said, eyebrows raised. "Oh yes, a key role. Do not discount yourself, Professor. Everything depends on you. At the end, we must be worthy. Our mission fails if we are not."

"I'm the least important of five now," I said. "I watch other people do things and think about taking more blood pressure meds."

"There's as much as you need in your room," he said airily, waving his hand, still admiring the cage. "And then we'll see if you were right. All those years ago."

"If I was right? I don't understand."

"My name, of course," he said.

"Your name?"

"Yes, Professor. You named me. Remember? You don't? More's the pity. It's all in Dr. Kilmar's notes. He was putting the finishing touches on his proposal, and you said he needed to christen the neuroframe. The proposal would sell better, I think you said. Kilmar couldn't think of anything, so you suggested Sisyphus."

"I have no memory of that."

"No? Well, I do. You said the ultimate task was hopeless. Man would always destroy himself. It was in his nature. Like Sisyphus with the rock."

"That's why you brought me here?"

"Yes. The names of things are so important. Whether we *can* save humankind is, of course, important. But *should* we? A different question entirely."

From down the hallway, a wrenching shattering noise broke the air. I turned from Kilmar and ran to Madeline's desk. The maglock had broken, and the mudheads poured through.

"Where's Mick?" Shlo asked.

I swiveled, searching for him.

"Dear God," Madeline said. "He's in the corridor."

Mick had disrobed and stood naked in front of the approaching horde, his hands held out in welcome. He looked like a god, and the mudheads stopped. He spoke to them, but I could not hear what he said. Just words and phrases. His hair fell down his back like a waterfall. Then he stopped speaking and closed his eyes. Everything was silent. The mudheads stared.

Something dripped onto Mick's hands. Then his arms, and head. Blood, from above. The ventilation shaft. Mick looked up, blinking.

I ran into the corridor, yelling at him to come back. But it was too late. The mudhead-laden ceiling crashed down on top of him. Then the mudheads devoured him. They clawed and bit and scraped and ripped. I lost sight of Mick, then a mudhead raised Mick's head high in the air with a chortling yowl. Mick's eyes blinked and blinked.

I felt hands on me. Shlo pulled me back inside the operations center, Krys brandishing her blade by my side. The mudheads finished with Mick, then surged toward the operations center with unnerving force and speed. Madeline closed the maglock behind us, beating the onrushing herd by only seconds.

"Can they get over top this room?" I yelled, terrified, looking up.

"No," Madeline said. "Our ventilation comes from Sissy's bunker. The only way they can get inside is through that door." She pointed to the maglock.

The mudheads writhed and wriggled outside the center, but, strangely, they did not push the door down. They held back. It's as if they were waiting. But waiting for what?

"They're bringing something forward," Madeline said, staring at her screens, her voice edged with fear and exhaustion, her hands shaking. "But I can't get a good look at it."

And then they were at the maglock. They shoved something up against it. Shoved it hard. A person, beaten to within an inch of its life. Then Madeline shrieked, and I saw. It was Patricia, bruised and bloody and bald. Naked and shivering. Grasping hands all over her. Ten, fifteen, twenty, maybe more. The mudheads were holding her tight to the maglock. Somehow they had found out I was here, and they had brought her along.

"Havens, you must open this door!" Patricia screamed. "You must do it now. They will kill me here and now if you do not. We can talk to them. We can reason with them. We can find a peaceful solution . . ."

I sank to my knees, no longer hearing her words. I sensed her voice like the sound wind makes outside at night. And I who had never cried, on this day I could not stop. My whole body wept and shook uncontrollably. Not only for Patricia's ordeal. Not only for the pain I had caused. But also for what I was being forced to do. What the Patricia-inside-my-head was instructing me to do. We were playing for time, Kilmar had said. Seconds mattered. But I did not matter, nor did Patricia. Humankind depended on me doing what was necessary. Quarrying every last moment from a deteriorating situation. Which meant I could not open the maglock under any circumstances.

Good-bye, Patricia, my love.

~~

I looked at my companions. Madeline, crying. Shlo, studying my anguish. Krys, anticipating the coming battle.

When I turned to the maglock, the mudheads held Patricia's head for me to see. *You did this*, they seemed to say. *It's your fault.* Her body had been ripped away. Then they tossed her head aside and rushed the maglock. It stood fast, but it wasn't going to last. Their force was overwhelming. I gestured Shlo to the cage. We retreated from the maglock so we would have room against our attackers. We spread out, Krys in the center. She was our bulwark, Madeline and I mere ornamentation.

Long and lean and undisturbed, Krys was magnificent. She shook her head and rolled her shoulders. Like she had been born to do this very specific thing on this very specific day. An avenging angel, she would face the mudhead horde that killed her family, and her only regret would be that she couldn't kill all of them.

I turned to the cage. Kilmar was placing Shlo in position. The mirrors were already moving, the lights flickering and dancing.

"So tell me this," I yelled at Kilmar. "Who are we fighting for? Where are you sending him?"

Kilmar spoke in a voice that reverberated throughout the operations center. "My preparations are now finished. I will send him to the Near East. The town of Nazareth. His name will be Jesus." Shlo stood naked in the cage with his eyes closed, feet apart, arms at his side. A moment twenty-five years in the making.

The final test of the Yahweh Project.

What are the odds, I thought, that this improbable fiction could save humankind?

"For Jesus of Nazareth!" Madeline proclaimed, holding her tasers high.

I hoped Shlo would open his eyes so I could look into them. One last time. For some reason I needed to see how he faced his mission. Was he ready? But his eyes stayed shut, and I turned around when I heard that awful crack. The one telling me the maglock was breaking apart. The one telling me my death was a few terrifying moments away.

The mudheads came at us in an engulfing wave, the way water pours from a wide-lipped pitcher. I swung and hacked and stabbed with my sword. They briefly pulled back to regroup. Krys was covered in blood, the tiniest half-smile on her face. I was drenched dark red myself. The floor was devilishly slick at my feet. Madeline was gone, her tasers on the floor. They had taken her, and she had never cried out. Krys and I repositioned ourselves to better protect the cage.

I glanced back. We had bought time, but we needed to buy more. Shlo was exactly as before, except his chin was raised, his head tilted back, his mouth open. But still there. Still with us in his flesh and bone and blood and breath. Kilmar mimicked the pose, as if wishing he could be the traveler.

The second wave exhausted me, and by the end Krys fought for both of us. She whirled and danced and leapt and pirouetted as she slaughtered mudheads. Their incessant wailing became a dirge. By the end the sword was so heavy in my hand I could hardly lift it. The floor was littered with dead and dying mudheads, their quivering body parts strewn like confetti on New Year's Eve. I staggered to turn around, and there was Shlo, again, infuriatingly, still in the cage. This time his feet were tight together, his arms outstretched, his head lolling forward, as if he were no longer conscious. We had to find a way to give him still more time.

Krys breathed heavily, but held her pose as if the first two waves had been nothing but a warm-up. Then, as the swarm at the door made a hideous hissing insect-like noise, she looked at me and smiled, and her eyes blew me the tiniest kiss. She was saying good-bye.

The third wave crashed down with brutal fury. The mudheads were fighting for survival. I lost my sword almost immediately, and they brought me low, first to one knee, then to my back. Their unseen hands pulled me apart while their teeth ripped me open. I struggled to my side, lowering my head to keep them from putting an arm under my chin. The pain was so sudden and sharp that I could taste it.

A sick bounce, like a dropped melon cracking on a hard kitchen floor, told me that Krys had fallen. With my last energy, I pushed myself sideways. I saw that face, her face, her broken head, her golden hair, one last time before the light drained from her eyes. And as I evaporated into my own death, I cast one final glance back to the cage. This time it was empty, and Kilmar too was gone. A million unleashed flashes littered the air, as if someone had diced an especially thick beam of starlight.

And I had a vision in that last drop of time. A man in a strange robe standing in front of a quiet lake, his hands outstretched, his eyes memorably and intensely green. He was speaking to people sitting on a hillside, and beyond those people the dusky night scattered infinite stars.

And oh, Patricia, I thought. In that light I can almost see my own soul.

Friedrich walked toward his office. The hallway was stark and antiseptic with white walls, white floors, and fluorescent lights flickering overhead. He was suspended outside of time and nature, with no trace of passing time other than the rhythm of his steps.

He noticed a diminutive, dark-haired young man waiting patiently in a chair, outside the door to his office. The man's right leg bounced, fanning the paper he held in his hand. Friedrich immediately saw him as a prospective student looking for some special access or opportunity. He decided to let him stew with his nerves a little. Friedrich continued walking past the young man and into his office.

Inside, Friedrich found another man sitting in an armchair. He was reading a magazine beneath the gaze of several oversized portraits of German Nobel scientists. "Mister President!" Friedrich said. "What an honor to have you come to see me in my office." Friedrich closed the door and advanced on the sitting man.

"Friedrich, I prefer to deliver bad news in private." The president of the university closed his magazine and stood.

"I don't understand, sir," Friedrich said.

"You must show something for all the money we have put into your program," said the president. "You are an excellent educator, but you must show a return on our investment."

"Of course, but I have published many times in the last year, and the theoretical progress has been tremendous."

"Theory does not pay for the lights or the water, Friedrich." The president moved toward the door, opening it enough so the young man in the hall could peer through.

"I am an excellent instructor and my work has brought in a dozen new masters and doctoral candidates," Friedrich argued.

"Friedrich, enough. Three months more. The Dean will report back to me on your progress." The president turned and left, not waiting for a response.

"Yes, sir, I understand," Friedrich replied.

The young man in the hall stood as the president walked past. He clutched a letter in one hand and a bound set of papers in the other. Stepping forward, he stole another furtive peek into Friedrich's office.

"Doctor, I wonder if I might introduce myself," said the young man sheepishly. He held a letter in front of him. "My name is Pascual Ben Gurion and I have come a very long way."

Friedrich impatiently snatched the paper away and read it. After what he hoped seemed like several minutes, he looked over the top of his wireframe glasses, addressing the younger man in a thick German accent, "A letter of introduction from Doctor Laurence Wolfe in Heidelberg no less. Impressive."

"Thank you, doctor."

"What is that in your hand?"

"My thesis, sir."

"And what brilliant contribution have you made to theoretical temporal physics?"

"I posit that, um…"

"Out with it," Friedrich snapped. "I haven't all day!"

"Well it seems silly and obvious, but I posit that in any time travel experiments it will be necessary to move the object into or away from the departure location. Otherwise the object will likely destroy itself by trying to occupy the same space. The paper is really just some mathematic proofs and thought experiments."

Friedrich snatched the thesis from the young man's hands and started thumbing through it. "Mmhmm, mhmm, of course you are right…"

The young man brightened.

"It is obvious, and something I have already considered in designing future experiments," said Friedrich.

This seemed to deflate the young man's prior excitement. Now his posture sagged.

But of course, the truth was that he hadn't considered this possibility. "Still," said Friedrich, "it is clear you have an eager and capable mind. I have money for a half-time assistant, and if you are willing to accept room and board in compensation, I could stretch that to full-time." After a brief pause he added, "Of course you will accept."

***

Pascual found himself living in a room just off of the laboratory. It was just an emptied janitorial closet, but that meant he had a sink. He had to use the shower and toilet in the back of the lab, put there as a safety precaution when the lab had first been built to serve the chemistry department.

Each morning he unlocked the lab and started the water for tea. Each night he meticulously copied notes from the various whiteboards around the room. He collated them and placed them in the doctor's office inbox.

Around the end of the third week, he offered a minor observation. He found a variable that seemed misplaced in one of the formulas derived from the work of the previous week. The equation was meant to describe power requirements to displace mass on a macroscale.

The doctor was ecstatic, he was nearly incoherent.

"Doctor, have I done something wrong?"

"No, young man, not at all." He placed his hand in a grandfatherly fashion on Pascual's cheek. "You have corrected an error, yours no doubt when you originally copied the equation last week, but nonetheless you have corrected it."

"I apologize if I made a mistake…"

"No need boy! No need! Your correction was perfectly timed. I think we can actually power a practical device, at least for objects under." He turned abruptly to a whiteboard and quickly erased what was there.

Pascual's breath caught. He raised his hand tentatively in protest. He had not copied those equations yet. But the professor did not seem to care.

"Yes, this means we should be able to power a device capable of displacing objects up to one hundred kilos. It is as if the universe has tailor made the answer."

"Doctor…"

"Come now, my boy, call me Friedrich when no one else is around."

***

The two men worked tirelessly, often alone, usually late into the night and through what other people thought of as weekends. While not exactly friends, they had an easy rapport. Pascual was like a muse to Friedrich. Years of frustration over answers just out of grasp evaporated as wisps of steam on the wind.

Only eleven weeks after they met, the two men were building a machine. They used no blueprints or instructions, to them it was intuitive, with just cursory references to the calculations found strewn about the lab, on papers, whiteboards, and sometimes the walls themselves.

Eventually, the core of the apparatus took shape, looking like a 1960s overhead projector used in classrooms around the world, but standing some two and a half meters tall. Just like those projectors, a large lens protruded near the top, but instead of pointing forward, it aimed at a spot on the floor nearly two meters away.

Attached about twenty centimeters from the base was a claw and tray on an articulated, retractable arm. This arm extended out to where the lens focused. The armature was designed to keep the target isolated from the ground.

***

"Friedrich," Pascual held up his glass, "this is an excellent wine."

"I found it on a pilgrimage along the Deutsche Weinstrasse in my homeland. It is the life's blood of the soil." The professor raised his glass in salute.

That night they toasted the completion of what, theoretically, would be a successful device for transporting objects through time.

"You know, Pascual, I do believe he is a very noble and efficient design." Friedrich motioned to the machine they had recently finished building.

"*He*, sir? Why do you say *he*?" Pascual poured them each the last of the second bottle of a 1950s vintage Spatburgunder wine.

"Women are capricious and unreliable. That is why it makes sense to name storms or even ships after women. But engineering and temporal physics are precise and predictable things, this manifestation then is masculine. This device is most definitely precise and perhaps the most powerful thing ever built."

Pascual shifted uncomfortably, staring down into his wineglass. He couldn't imagine the professor had many lady friends. "I do not think inanimate things have a gender," Pascual said. "For me, they are just things."

"Well of course you would not understand." The professor snorted. "But no matter, on Monday we will apply your maths to Philipp and make—or maybe remake—history."

Clearly the machine now had a name in addition to a gender.

"Is that wise?" Pascual said. "Remaking history, I mean."

"I have no idea, young man, but one is honor bound to try and correct mistakes of the past. To aid the successes of the righteous. To prevent the senseless deaths of good people."

"I am not sure I follow. How can you know your outcome will be better?"

"I have faith in the vision."

"Was not Herr Lenard mistaken though, about so many things?"

Friedrich stared hard at Pascual, coldly appraising him. "What makes you think I speak of a vision of Doctor Lenard?"

Embarrassed, Pascual fumbled. "I, um." He drained the wine from his glass. Pascual made a show of seeing nothing left in the bottle. "I believe, Friedrich, that it is time for me to say good night."

***

For a few days, things were tense between the two men. Suspicion that Pascual might harbor some ulterior motives nagged at Friedrich, but eventually he dismissed them. Pascual was not clever enough to truly deceive for so long.

For his part Pascual ignored the strain on their relationship. He knew he would be present at a historic moment in time. He had no doubt that the professor would be successful in moving objects through time, and ultimately people. That is why he had come here, to be present, to witness it himself, to maybe have some small role. A little tension was not the worst thing that could have happened.

"Pascual, be sure the highspeed camera is set properly," ordered the professor.

This day they conducted the sixth experiment in jumping a melon back slightly in time. The first four times did not appear to be successful in doing anything other than flattening the fruit. It had been Pascual's suggestion that they only try and move fractions of a second at first, certainly no more than one or two seconds. He had shown in a few mathematic thought experiments that they would better be able to control for unforeseen variables by reducing the time.

"Check the armature one more time while you are there!" The professor's voice echoed from outside the isolation chamber.

Pascual did as he was told and secured the door on his way out.

⁣⁣*

Friedrich slept fitfully that night. His dreams haunted by German Nobel winners taunting him for letting

German Science down. In his dream he screamed back that it was they that let Germany down. He did not wake until noon on Saturday, and when he did he was not rested.

He called his assistant from the computer at his bedside. "Pascual, perhaps we must try something different, get me some metal and stone objects, let us see if those can withstand the movement through time."

He paused, listening to Pascual's objections about working over yet another weekend.

"Do not question me, just obey. I must get this right, there is so much to do. I will be in the laboratory in one hour. Have what I need ready."

His age was beginning to remind him that time was not infinite, at least not for a man. His knees ached as he rose from his bed.

He poured water from a bone-white porcelain pitcher into a matching bowl. The set had been buried in a trunk in the back of the storeroom of a Turkish antiques dealer, who set up shop in sight of the famous bridge of Arnhem, in the Netherlands. Splashing water on his face, Friedrich stared into his own eyes staring back from the mirror. *Though the body is not, time is infinite. To control time is to have all the time I will ever need.*

***

Pascual knew the funding was running short and that Friedrich must show progress or lose the lab and future funding for this research. He would be left with lecturing and writing until he could find new funding, if he could find it. But even that did not seem to explain the change in behavior. Friedrich was always superior in his demeanor, condescending in his discourse, but now he was frenzied and driven, as if he was being chased by some demon.

"Pascual, set the iron sphere in place, please."

The assistant did as he was bid. But when they secured the chamber and ran the program, the result was the same as for the aluminum, the steel, the granite, and the marble. Nothing.

Nothing happened. The machine cycled, but the objects stayed in place. Nothing appeared before or after the sequence. The objects refused to move through time.

"*Scheisse!*" Friedrich cursed.

***

Friedrich had been flustered by the failures over the weekend. So far, they had tried organic and inorganic materials, and only the organic materials were affected by the machine. Monday afternoon found Friedrich sitting alone talking to the portraits of his German predecessors, in particular, Philipp Lenard, master of the cathode ray.

"It must be that fool Pascual. He must have done something wrong." But Friedrich knew that was not the case. "I must uncover the problem. I must succeed. I will. Your mistakes must be remedied."

A knock at the door startled him from his contemplations.

"Enter," he barked, more a command than a response.

"Good afternoon doctor," the Dean of the Institute of Sciences approached the large desk in the center of the office.

"Dean, my apologies, I was lost in thought."

"Yes, yes, I am sure you were." A meaningful pause hung in the air. "You have much to consider. Your funding runs out next week, and I am afraid that the board and the president of the university are not inclined to fund your research any further."

"I understand, but I believe I can sway faculty and the board if you will indulge me. I would like to give a presentation Wednesday, after which I believe they will wish me to continue."

"Schedule the auditorium, and make it worthwhile," said the dean. He turned to leave but paused. "Include the students. They need to see that research must and does bear results."

***

The following day Friedrich and Pascual repeated the experiments with the melons. They had isolated the experiments from external factors, even offsetting the forward and backwards experiments twelve hours to avoid any unforeseen impact from the different settings on the machine. Mornings they tried to send things to the past, evenings to the future. But in each case, they smashed the melons.

Time ran out on them. The morning dawned outside their little universe of concrete block walls, nearly incoherent scribbles, and slaughtered melons. Friedrich had to prepare for his do or die presentation, and Pascual was forced to stand by helpless.

***

Wednesday evening the auditorium was standing room only. Some students came, though they did not need to, out of curiosity about the eccentric professor. Faculty from other departments came to see what it looks like when one's funding runs out and they have to beg for supper.

Introductions were made. A brief history of time travel in popular culture set the tone, perhaps unintentionally.

117

"It is a worthwhile question. Maybe, the only worthwhile question," Friedrich waxed passionately this evening at a podium of the Central Institute of Sciences in the University of Brasilia. "Can we go back in time to deliberately change events? Can we change the injustices of the past?"

Pascual had heard it all before. He knew the professor would figure out the problems. Despite smashing to pieces, several melons had travelled a few moments forward in time, and several a few moments back. Everything else was just scale. Tonight was the night Friedrich would persuade the men who controlled the purse strings to come to a practical demonstration, and to continue to fund their research.

"There are varying theories as to the plasticity of time, regarding our impact should we acquire the ability to travel in time."

Students in the audience began to yawn. Aside from those who had come out of curiosity, many were only here for the few extra credits it earned them. And for some, that was the difference between passing and failing. The attending faculty were also bored. But they were too professional or stubborn to show it. The lecture had been arranged last minute, so it had little in the way of distractions or entertaining extras such as music or interactive media projected on to a giant screen. It was simply a serious and monotone man, trying to explain a complex and esoteric branch of physics to a captive audience. And Wednesday evening was not exactly an ideal time to hold such an event at a university where classes began at 7:30 in the morning.

"Some believe the answer is short, and that the answer is no," Friedrich said from the stage. "For them, if an event is the target of your travel, or the impetus for your invention, and you alter it, you would not therefore invent time travel, nor be inspired to make the trip. Thus, at best, you have an infinite loop cordoned off from the general thread of time."

Pascual could see that Friedrich sensed a growing impatience in the audience. The tempo of the delivery picked up.

"Others believe that by altering an event you create a branch in the river of time. A separate stream that, depending on the severity of the disruption, may return eventually to the primary river, or, in extreme instances, continue on a separate and no less real course."

His voice made clear his desperation. He wanted to make them understand the potential, to see the glory to be achieved.

"Of course, this is all just theoretical, until someone is able to demonstrate motion in both directions of time other than at the subatomic level."

They were all starting to breathe through their mouths.

Friedrich slammed his fist down. "TODAY!" He paused, seeming to enjoy the jerking heads and startled expressions. He leaned forward, jutting out his chin. "Today I bring you proof we CAN travel through time."

Pascual rose from his seat unnoticed. He ducked his head and moved from the glow of the stage toward the back of the audience, behind the mass of faces.

"LIGHTS!" Friedrich shouted dramatically, hoping the crowd was finally captivated.

A video projection above the podium lit up as the lights faded. He saw himself on screen in a lab coat, adjusting the lens of the camera in slow motion, before walking first to the right, off camera, then across to the left, closing a door behind himself. A moment later, in that closed room, a melon appeared, smashed on a smooth concrete floor, a pink numeral '6' still legible among the bits of rind. Seconds later, a robotic arm moved out over the melon, holding a melon with an identical pink '6' painted on it. Then the melon vanished.

"Fake!" A lone anonymous voice called out in the hushed dark.

A second video started. The tableau repeated, but this time there was no smashed melon. The arm extended, a new melon, pink '13,' rested in the arm, and vanished. The arm withdrew immediately and again on the floor appeared a smashed melon bearing the same number '13.'

The lights came back up. "Fraud!" The voice this time from a different part of the crowd. Friedrich hung his head knowing they were not truly ready for this all-to-public reveal. Tonight was supposed to be about creating interest in the senior faculty to see a live demonstration, tantalizing them with words about "promising results." He searched the crowd for his assistant, seeking some support, but Pascual was not in sight.

"This is a joke!" yet another voice shouted. Friedrich understood that video could be faked, and his claims probably did seem outrageous.

And to be fair, Friedrich still did not understand why the melons were smashed to the ground.

The crowd began to laugh. Friedrich grew agitated. "Tomorrow, hours from now, I will travel back in time, to this location, to a few minutes from now, with tomorrow's newspaper."

Friedrich glanced at his watch to mark the time. "Behold!" He waved his hand to a spot next to the podium. But nothing happened. He did not appear.

The room erupted in even louder laughter. Half empty coffee cups and water bottles were flung on to the stage as the audience made a dash for the doors, eager to tell others about how a distinguished professor of theoretical physics went completely insane in front of two hundred witnesses.

***

Pascual found himself pouring the last of another bottle of German red wine into his glass again. This time not in celebration, but in apparent defeat.

Friedrich drank his wine in one go, then threw the crystal glass against the wall. "I will NOT be defeated. I WILL succeed."

The assistant stayed quiet, for the first time in months totally unsure of what would come next.

"Pascual, tomorrow we will move the device to the stage I used last night. We will run the sequence and I will project myself into the past, to that very moment."

Pascual raised a finger and began to speak. "I ah…"

"Say nothing, just be here early, and tell no one."

"Yes, sir." There was nothing left to discuss. Pascual left his glass on the table, the wine unfinished.

***

The next morning the dean found Friedrich and Pascual in their lab, dismantling their device. Both men were dressed casually. Pascual in jeans and a Time Tunnel t-shirt, Friedrich in linen pants, a cotton shirt and leather sandals.

"Gentlemen, I am surprised, but pleased to see that you anticipated my visit," said the dean. "Your positions are secure for the remainder of the academic year, but, as you obviously realize, we cannot fund this folly any longer. Best we put it behind us. A clever joke made in bad judgment, yes?"

He turned to go, but paused, looking over his shoulder. "Do be sure to dress more appropriately when you are finished with that work will you? It is only Thursday morning after all."

The dean left and the two men, master and student, silently went back to work. Each piece of the deceptively simple and elegant looking machine was taken apart with haste, but care. A compressed version of putting the machine together, but in reverse. Placed in a cart, the components were shifted to the auditorium that hosted the embarrassing events of the previous evening. Each piece was then put back together without reference to any designs. The only modification, a metal pad on the stage floor in the place of the arm that held the melons.

***

In the back of the auditorium, a janitor loaded several large bags of refuse into a wheelbarrow, the last of the missiles from the previous night.

"We are not ready yet," Pascal intoned, knowing it fell on deaf ears. "If I do not try now I will not appear then."

"But…"

"Yes, I know, I did not appear." Friedrich gestured impatiently with the morning paper. "And to understand why, I must complete the effort."

Friedrich opened the back panel of the device. He referred to his watch, closed his eyes and made some quick mental calculations before adjusting several graduated but unlabeled dials within the belly of the beast.

Pascual pondered for a moment. "I do not pretend to understand all that you have reasoned to get even this far."

The doctor moved to the front of the device and made adjustments to the large crystal lens. "Yes, Pascual, that is to be expected." Friedrich stepped onto the metal pad and handed his glasses to the younger man. "It is not for the inferior man to understand the designs of his betters. Now, please step back and throw the switch."

The assistant did as he was directed, and the professor vanished.

"I did not pretend…" the assistant began to say.

***

In an instant, twelve hours earlier, Friedrich Heidler was falling, stung by a biting cold that snatched his breath away. He squeezed the newspaper, dated 30 April 2020, tight in his hand. All around it was dark except for a blue and white ball, the size of a full moon, shining in the distance. His vision went blurry, his chest spasmed for air that was not there. His last conscious thought, *Of course.*

***

Back in the next day's auditorium, Pascual finished, "you failed to understand celestial mechanics. Your great uncle Adolf and his delusions are not just seventy-five years, but also seventy billion kilometers, in the past. And that is where they will stay."

Pascual opened the access panel on Philipp and reversed two wires, ensuring that anyone who attempted to replicate the now discredited experiments would only get inside-out melons for their troubles. With no blueprints, they would likely never figure out why.

Then Pascual Ben Gurion vanished back to the future.

ISA Mercon
International Space Agency Warship
Jovian Equatorial Belt - 2061 C.E.

"This is ISA Warship *Mercon* directing unidentified vessel moving on Jovian spin-wise vector twenty-three degrees south by minus thirty-eight degrees ecliptic. You are to make your instant elevation cloud top prime and move to a stationary position at the coordinate packet side-banded to this transmission. Comply and prepare to be boarded or you will be fired upon."

Screaming winds of the eternal storm managed to penetrate even to the bridge, casting an unnatural aura over the encounter. As a captain of wavedrive class starships for the past six years, there was very little that surprised the *Mercon's* captain. This chance discovery was proving the exception. He didn't like this damned planet. They'd lost too many vessels here in the relatively calm upper reaches of this killer's atmosphere. However, he was a professional and his concerns rarely tainted the clarity of command. "Ensign Blover, how is it their presence was not known to us earlier?"

The ensign never looked up from his station. "Sir, they are near impossible to detect much less secure a lock on. Most likely they were floating with zero relative motion to the surrounding storms centers. Our sensors first classified the bogie designated Sierra One as a floating proto-biomass. AI classification currently rates their hull type as 'unknown' but most definitely synthetic."

Lieutenant Casowry broke into the subsequent moment of silence. "Action, sir?"

The captain looked with surprise at his executive officer before softly replying, "Patience Lieutenant."

The planet they call 'Jupiter,' is nearly three times the mass of all other planets and debris in the solar system combined. *Mercon* was pushing its way through the uppermost reaches of a swirling storm of brown and red cyclones that, even here on the edge of space, surrounded the starship while extending deadly fingers of hot, radiation-laden gas out to the stars far enough to fit several Earth-sized planets beneath their arches. Lightning played within this chaos, running from cloud-tip to cloud-tip, leaving a strange flickering glow upon the bridge.

The captain's response was firm. "Make ready tactical torpedoes. Ensign, bring us …"

The unknown ship was gone. It didn't accelerate. Not even the quickness of a wavedrive could have accounted for such an instant disappearance. The ensign took pride in knowing his job. "Signal is lost but there were two milliseconds of secondary electron emission in the path they took through the storm tops."

"Lay in the course, Ensign," commanded the captain. "All ahead but safe harbor."

"Aye aye, sir, all ahead, safe harbor. We are in pursuit."

The tiniest of shudders shook the ship and the storm clouds were gone. They found themselves in a channel carved into the cloud cover of the great planet. "Sir, I have a clear residual graviton stream to follow."

"Retain unknown classification. Continue pursuit. Fire missiles as you lock on."

"Aye aye, sir. Fire missiles as we lock on."

"All missiles, release success."

Then a minute later. "All munitions reporting negative impact, sir."

"Ready tactical nuclear one, three and five. Fire as you bear."

This required authorization. "Nuclear release approved, tactical officer confirmation."

Sailing onward to the center of a cloud-free channel wide enough to float an Earth-sized planet, the unidentified starship's path became obvious. In the distance, towering high above even the fearsome cloud-tops of this gas giant, lay a swirling cyclone of angry red and black clouds. They were on a side-approach to the Great Red Spot of Jupiter, a storm column laced with high energy discharges, glowing with the photon emission of ions accelerated to near lightspeed. An eternal tornado, wide enough to pass three Earth-sized planets down its gullet without touching its churning outer edges.

"Well that explains the trough we follow," the captain said to no one in particular. "We're in the cloud-wash of that thing."

Fear laced the ensign's announcement. "Sir, we have AI confirmed detonation from weapon's release but no noticeable effects, not even in the surrounding cloud banks.

"Shall I break off, sir?"

"Ensign, remember your station. Refrain from suggesting actions."

"Intruder visual, sir."

The captain pulled up a greatly magnified image with the ship's AI enhancing its smallest details. Directly ahead lay the roaring storm column, its image crisp and clear but the bogie remained out of focus, although obviously still on course. He watched it slam into the storm wall leaving little more indication of its collision than a pebble thrown into a raging river.

"Follow bogie," said the captain. "Lay in a course for that exact entry point. Sound collision."

Beads of sweat on Lt. Casowry's forehead were the only indication of his fear. "Sir, that's obviously not a Mars Confederation vessel. I suggest we break off."

White, straining knuckles dug furrows into the arms of the command seat but not a word sounded on the bridge as the ship flung itself against the storm wall. A last second's hallucination materialized from a spot ahead in the form of a black fog growing in their path. The shuttle hatch alarm sounded and, faster than the ensign could react, an unnatural fog enveloped their ship. They slammed into the wall.

***

A million shards of human-manufactured materials flared in a brown smear on the inside shell of the cyclone. It existed for less than a second before a smudge of black fog materialized, somehow retaining an oblate cohesion as it churned and boiled in its emergence from the swirling wall of clouds.

Clear of the storm wall, the cloud dissipated and, in its place, a silvery shuttle took form. Not the smooth sleek shape of a starship, but a boxy, sharp-cornered, purely functional design. The shuttle's AI began repairs even as the fog dissipated. Power levels stabilized from the overload and ventilation pushed a life-sustaining high-oxygen and nitrogen mix through the cabin.

ISA Lieutenant Nichols Alsoi was the first to recover. Training kicked in and his eyes called up shuttle status, a moment later he nodded and turned to look for the others. Words formed unconsciously on his lips. "Only four?"

Engineer Jack Arlow groaned. "Not exactly my first thoughts after having gone through all that. Where's ... Hey, Jerry, you made it!"

Spacer Jerimiah Johnson was on the deck resting cross-legged in a corner, the body of a slim brunette lay across his lap while he held his hand to her head. "Sara needs help. She skull-butted something and has a broken leg."

"First time I've ever seen the great 'Sara Prakset, Journalist' with her mouth shut," whined the engineer.

Alsoi's eyebrows knotted in disapproval. "Enough of that, Mr. Arlow. Get up and make yourself useful. We aren't out of this yet.

"It appears that only four of us made it. I can't locate the *Mercon* or any other shuttles."

Jack Arlow let out a low whistle then held his head from the pain that flared as he rose. "Cheez on a crutch. Four? Only four of us out of a crew of four hundred and thirty-eight?"

"Plus, the journalist," Jerry added. "Hey, you got the forward display working. Good job. But where's all the jetsam? Shouldn't we be in the middle of the debris field?"

The forward wall display panned its view as Alsoi replied, "Good question. Nothing around and look where we find ourselves."

"We ain't in Kansas no more," Jack grumbled.

Jerry looked at the engineer. "Where the heck does he come up with these sayings?"

"Clam up and take a look around." The lieutenant's command voice filled the cabin. Their shuttle traveled within a cylinder, or more accurately, a long tube. Its sides were rotating angry walls of discharge-laced storm clouds that managed to reveal a small circle of far-off stars at one distant end of the tube and fade off into some invisible destination far below.

"Think that's sexy?" Jack said. "Look over here where my marker's pointing."

In the near distance lay the mysterious vessel they'd fired upon. It tracked as close to the storm wall as possible as it came on in an indirect but obvious approach pattern. Eventually, the strange vessel began to take shape. It was black, not a dull light-absorbing black, but shiny with fine rainbow Lissajous ribbons of light dancing over the skin. Its surface took on details, sleek like a teardrop at times, then rippled like the shallow guidance channels of a hypervelocity missile before transforming on to a thousand other patinas. Then a spinning black jet emerged from its side, visible only by portions of the distant storm wall it occluded and the play of rainbows across its surface. The cloud expanded, increasing its density as it neared.

"Oh shit, this is it. No more for us, Betty," Jack whined as he backed off from the approaching threat. Like a bad dream, it was upon them with impossible speed, spreading out until it engulfed the shuttle. "Cheez, Lieutenant, get us outta here!"

Alsoi was already lunging for the controls, but just as rapidly, a patch of black mist entered the cabin. It defied the solid walls of their shuttle, as though the plastisteel barriers were no more tangible than a sunbeam. The mist settled over the control panel, where it solidified to a hard, silvery surface.

"Pry it off," said Jack.

"I'm not going anywhere near that stuff. You too, back off." Alsoi's eyes moved to the wall display. "Even if we could run, there's nowhere to go unless you want to try that stormfront again. Besides, it hasn't tried to hurt anyone so far."

"That so? How about what it did to our ship?"

Controls blocked, the mist somehow permitted the visuals of the wall display to continue as it drew the shuttle toward the mysterious black object. As they approached, they began to appreciate its huge proportions. A portion of the ship's black skin lightened as their shuttle approached the great vessel. To their surprise, the ship's skin enveloped them, sucking the entire shuttle in like waves of water flowing over a rock passing through a waterfall.

Then the mist was gone.

Their shuttle was now in a huge chamber that was obviously a docking bay, complete with light gray walls and no clear source of illumination. Alsoi noticed the control panel was now free and lunged for it.

"Nothing, no response at all," said Alsoi. "AI's dead. Can't even fire the bootstrap sequencer.

"Quick, weapons locker …"

The shuttle's hatch shot open without the expected sound of sliding metal or shush of air pressure equalizing to a new environment. Two humanoids entered. Their general shape is where the resemblance stopped. They had no external distinguishing marks, but were shining black like the ship itself with the same narrow, contiguous rainbow patterns dancing across their surfaces.

A deep voice, amplified and obviously accustomed to command, rang out at them. "I'm Gunnery Sergeant Arlington. You can call me Gunny or Sergeant Arlington. We'll do the rest of the formalities later. You and you, leave now with the corporal. Do as Prachert instructs or you will suffer for it. We have no time to play around.

"You," said the other figure, a woman's voice, "the cute one holding the girl, continue as you are. Hold her and do not move no matter what happens in the next few moments."

Apparently the shock of hearing his own language didn't stop Jerimiah. He opened his mouth, looking like he was about to object. But then he must have thought better of it at the last second, because he clamped his mouth shut, giving a small nod of compliance.

"Good, not as dumb as you look," boomed the voice of the gunnery sergeant. "Now, don't move." A fine black mist materialized midair between the menacing figure and Jerry. It thickened as it drifted with the grace of pollen on an air current over to the still unconscious journalist. Jerry stiffened the slightest bit, but caught himself before the figure could release a reprimand. The dry mist settled, covered the injured journalist's leg then disappeared.

"Not good." Jerry twitched in spite of himself as the sergeant's low voice surrounded the spacer. "It's a spiral compound fracture, the girl's lucky to have passed out.

"I'm gonna sedate her and immobilize the leg until we can get Doc to look it over," said the gunnery sergeant. "Lucky for her the doc's with us, never really trust autodocs myself." Once again, more mist appeared and settled onto the injured leg, this time encasing it in a thick black sheaf. A second patch of mist followed and floated around them, avoiding the spacer as it encased the girl and gently lifted her body.

"You waitin' for Sunday, Spacer?" said the gunnery sergeant. "Release and step back."

Jerry jumped at the command then scrambled back. "Thanks Sarge, I was gettin' a bit stiff."

"Get outside with the other two and I ain't your Sarge."

"They listening out there, Prachert?"

"Aye, sir," replied the other figure.

"Okay, on yer feet," said the gunnery sergeant. "All of you, you hiding any weapons?"

"No?" The gunny hesitated a moment. "How about that, they're honest.

"Okay, Prachert," the gunny said to the second figure. "We can unsuit." The black figures dissolved in an instantly dissipating puff of black smoke, revealing a man and a woman.

Jack, ever the wise guy, commented to Jerry, jerking his head toward the woman. "Hey, it's a girl!"

She frowned. "Last two times I checked, Spacer. Now …"

The gunny's growl interrupted. "That will be enough from you, buddy, and you too, Prachert. He meant nothing by it."

Alsoi decided it was time he introduce himself. "I'm Lieutenant Nichols Alsoi of the ISA *Mercon*."

"Don't really care, Lieutenant," replied the gunny. "You guys fired on us. Far as I'm concerned, you ain't friends. You are uninvited intruders and more trouble than you are worth, but I'll let the captain deal with that. Now button up, you ain't gonna learn anything from us. We have orders. Follow me, don't touch anything and don't try to run. Prachert, fall in behind and make sure our invalid doesn't float off."

A passthrough formed in the bulkhead from a section where no obvious portal existed an instant before. They entered a decorated, almost ornate passageway, quite unlike any military vessel Alsoi had ever served on. The deck looked like hard steel but was soft and comfortable underfoot. Nearly all bulkheads had active picture-like wall displays but without any obvious circuitry. Turning a bend, they passed through a panorama of the churning storm tunnel. No visible sign of their shuttle or ship remained.

"It's gone, Lieutenant," came Prachert's voice from behind. "Your shuttle is downtime by now at …"

"Prachert, button it or you are on report." The gunny had just enough time to blast out the words when two of the strangest but also most beautiful animals Alsoi had ever seen came racing around the corner. They charged in. Massive, shoulder high, muscular roadrunners but sporting arms and hands instead of wings. They screeched to a halt not two paces ahead of the group. One looked at the gunny, flashing a set of sharp white teeth set in a broad, flexible muzzle. The other whipped a multicolored tail with a spatula-like plume of feathers at its tip forward to balance its abrupt stop. It turned to the stunned lieutenant, staring at him with cold, golden eyes and opened its mouth when …

"You birdbrains were told to stay outta here!" shouted the gunny. "Not a peep outa ya. Get back upcountry."

The animals turned, looked at each other and decided to leave. They were gone in an instant but not before leaving a defiant call of something that sounded faintly reminiscent of birdsong.

"I swear this should not be this difficult," said the gunny. "Lucky for me this is where I dump you. Inside. Now.

"Stay put until we return. We've got business, but it shouldn't take long. Look around to your heart's content but don't make a mess or you'll end up working it off. Food, entertainment and terminal access to ship's services are available. It's a bit different from what you're used to but most of you are smart people. Figure it out. There's no lock on the door but, once again, stay put. Even if you decide to ignore our hospitality, there's nowhere to go and you just might find yourselves breathing vacuum."

They were pushed into the room and the door closed without further ceremony, then the gunny reopened it. "Oh yeah. Doc's on his way down to help yer friend. Be nice to the Doc, you may need him someday. Never piss off one of those guys, ain't healthy."

The door closed and Jerimiah started exploring the room, then stopped. "Hey, what'd he mean 'almost all of you'? Was that an insult?"

Their quarters were obviously empty office space with a forward waiting room, a middle room with a plain desk and behind it a longer one with four beds and a small mess-station. Jerry tried the door and nearly fell over himself when it opened.

"Hey, Lieutenant," Jerry said. "We're outta here. They really didn't lock the door."

Alsoi walked over, silently pointing to a small strip blinking along the edge of the door frame. "They'd know and I don't think they really care. However, our warden might be a bit upset with you and I'm not sure I'd want to piss off the gunny. Anyways, not yet.

"Like he said, where can we go? You all saw this ship? This thing's huge, a battlecruiser. We'd be lucky to find our way back. Now, before you say a word, I can see it in your eyes, don't even dream about the four of us taking over. We have to wait and see what happens."

The room announced, "Doctor Silas Metrix requests entry."

"Come in," Alsoi replied. A fit, deeply tanned young man of perhaps twenty years entered.

"Hello, apparently a Ms. Prakset has a compound fracture. We also discovered a second, more serious problem. We'll deal with them but before I start on Ms. Prakset, since this is the first time you'll be coming in-system, I'd like to take a scan of each of you. This will take no time at all. Who's first?"

"One minute, please," said Alsoi. "Are you a doctor or just an intern? You look awfully young. Where did you get Sara Prakset's medical records? It's obvious, she has a compound spiral fracture of the tibia. That's not a quick fix."

"I'm busy … oh, since you're new here. Yes, I am a medical doctor. Have been one for years. I learned about Ms. Prakset's fracture and other problems from the NullBot survey performed earlier. They've already started treatment by ensuring there is full blood flow to the foot and no air exposure to the open wound. Now, if you will let me start, I'd like to complete my work here. There's much to do.

"Now, all of you, please stand still a moment. That's … it. All done."

"What survey?" Alsoi asked. "And what's a 'nollbrot?'"

"Ask one of the others later or, better still, look it up for yourself. Ah, I see she's still asleep. Looks like she's going to wake in a minute, thirty-seven seconds. We'll spare her the pain." The doctor seemed to concentrate on a distant section of the bulkhead for a moment.

"Done. Now, allow me to practice my trade."

The doctor held out his hands, palm-to-palm, and that apparently universal black mist formed between them. Then it floated over, thickening as it went, until it formed a liquid coating from Sara's knee to the tip of her toes.

"Very good, we'll let them work a moment. In the meantime, I'll address the genetic disorder. This is a GenoBot projector, I'm sure you've heard of them so don't become alarmed. I'll just …"

Alsoi leaned forward, grabbing the young man's hand. "One moment, Doctor."

"Oh, still not sure? I'm sorry. It's quite safe. An everyday procedure, I assure you. In any case, it's done and I'd really rather you restrain yourself from touching me again."

Alsoi let go. "Doctor, please explain your actions with greater clarity and move a little slower. This is all new to …" Then Alsoi stopped mid-sentence, noticing something moving over the journalist's leg and foot. The fracture's bulge moved, twisted, pulled, and realigned the foot. The patient never seemed to notice.

"Nicely timed," said the doctor. "The young lady had a predisposed genetic tendency to late cerebral cancer that would have begun causing problems in roughly seven years. We've fixed that and added some longevity maintenance and … I'm done. Good day." The doctor rose and moved for the door.

Alsoi rushed in front of him, remembering his request not to be touched. "What about the leg? I thought …"

A puzzled expression flooded over Dr. Metrix and he twisted to look back at his patient. The journalist was sitting up, a smile on her face as though she'd just awakened from a good night's sleep.

"Why're you all staring?" she slurred a bit as she tried to stand, then seemed to remember. "The attack, what happened?"

"There, you see? All is well." Dr. Metrix flashed his most professional smile and left.

***

Scarcely a half hour passed when their door opened and GySgt. Arlington barged into the room. "Heads-up, people, your chief babysitter's on deck. We have an upcoming event Captain Tafton wants you to see. Non-attendance is not an option. Follow me."

The gunnery sergeant led them all out and down a new passage. He stayed silent, apparently not in a talkative mood. Alsoi mused that if the gunny considered this babysitting, he wasn't surprised. NCOs were alike no matter what service they were in or the title they carried.

Scenes of a beautiful tropical jungle filled the passageway's bulkheads, even playing across the deck and overheads, making their trek more like a stroll down a manicured woodland trail, mildly scented in exotic aromas. Jerry, Jack and Sara let out noises of amazement as they took in the scene. Breezes washed over them, a bit warmer than Alsoi would have liked but somehow calming. He was wondering why they kept it so warm when they came to a broad passage holding the first of several glideways.

He'd seen glideways before in the orbiting Skyport but those were crude compared to the simple elegance of the moving deck they now trod upon. Many people were on the transport, traveling in both directions. This glideway, somehow keyed to the individual, allowed some people to simply stand while moving lazily down the corridor. Other travelers sped by, moving quickly whether they walked, jogged or chose to stand in place and let the glideway do all the work. At one point, Alsoi was astonished to see a traveler rise above deck level and disappear into the overhead like an apparition passing through a wall.

He stopped to stare in wonder of how this might operate and thought, *Solid walls apparently have no meaning to these people. Such technology. Why do they all carry sidearms? Come to think of it, even that doctor sported one, an unheard-of practice when on-board ship even in a combat situation.*

Where are we going? I'd sure like to move a bit faster than this.

Suddenly he accelerated past the Sergeant.

"Yo, just where do ya think you're going, Mac?" said the gunnery sergeant. "Lieutenant or not, you are to follow me. That translates to, no charging ahead."

"Sorry, Sergeant. Guess I got carried away."

A snicker rose from someone behind. Alsoi guessed either Jack or Jerry was laughing at him, but didn't turn to see who the culprit was. He also noted that Sara was staying uncharacteristically quiet.

They entered a new passageway displaying a lightly wooded ridgeline. Off in the near distance was a cliff edge bordering a broad gorge. In its center, a churning river, the obvious creator of the gorge. Huge animals moved along the valley floor. Some were thick-skinned like furry elephants but most looked like fluffy or brightly feathered birds of huge proportions. There were very few wild animal screams, all Alsoi heard was birdsong. *Well, not exactly the familiar patterns of home.* These calls and their melody were so much more complex then birdsong.

Then, down in the river … he began to ponder.

A hard tap on the shoulder brought him back to the reality of GySgt. Arlington, who said, "Yeah, I know. A thousand questions but not yet. We get off just ahead."

Passageway walls here transformed to exotic wood paneling. Unusual music filled the air, quite pleasant but strange. Something Alsoi had never seen on a starship lay ahead, a set of ornate wood doors that opened as they neared the end of the passageway.

Their group entered a broad room with subdued lighting. The gunnery sergeant directed them over to what looked like an honest-to-goodness lounge area. Then a human waiter approached, thoroughly astounding Alsoi, this was a luxury typically restricted to the most expensive restaurants on Earth.

The waiter smiled and said, "Welcome to the Nolen Lounge." Then he looked at Alsoi expectantly. Shocked, Alsoi discovered he suddenly knew everything on the menu. He glanced at the sergeant and was about to ask if he could order, when the non-com spoke with obvious amusement. "Of course you can order. We have time. The captain decided to remain on the bridge until we exit and is sending someone in his place. For now, I suggest you keep your eyes tuned to what's happening outside. You've been through it before but you ain't never seen it this way. Look outside. See those glowing strings just twisting and spinning down the center of the tunnel? Helps if ya squint and look to the side a bit rather than right at 'em. Dr. Freeman says it's some kind of photon emission from gravity particles snapping into different energy states or something like that."

Their vessel traveled inside the cyclone walls of the long storm-tunnel. It was impossible to determine the direction or speed of their movement. But they did seem to be on an inward course toward the tunnel's center. Alsoi stared across to the center of the storm-tube and could see nothing until he looked away. His peripheral vision caught a glimpse of a pair of very faint strings, glowing under a white-blue light as they spun, twisting about each other off into the distance following the very center of this massive tube formed by the spinning storm clouds.

"Mind if I join you, Sergeant?" A middle-aged woman appeared, touching the sergeant's shoulder ever so lightly.

He stood, almost stumbled as he turned to the new speaker. The gunny looked uncharacteristically nervous, "Ugh, no. Of course not, ma'am. I'm sorry, I didn't know you'd be here."

"Now, Trent, this is silly. How many times must I ask you to relax? Lord knows we've known each other long enough." Then, turning to the others, she smiled. "Hi, I'm Hailey Sharpe. I'm sorry for all you've had to go through. We'll try and make your transition as enjoyable as possible."

Alsoi and Jack Arlow had taken a cue from the sergeant and were already standing. Alsoi glanced over at the still nervous gunny and raised his eyebrows, silently mouthing, 'Trent?' For a flashing second, the man stiffened then smiled wickedly at the lieutenant.

Alsoi tried to pull Jerry out of his seat to his feet, so he could show Ms. Sharpe some respect. But the man did not budge. Alsoi didn't even bother trying to move Sara, who probably needed to rest after her injuries.

He turned to Ms. Sharpe. "I have no idea what 'transition' we may be taking but I'm Lieutenant Nichols Alsoi." He gave a knowing smile to the sergeant, obviously they shared embarrassing first names. At that point, he made a mental note, noticing even Hailey was armed.

He decided it was time he introduced his crew to Ms. Sharpe. "Allow me to introduce Journalist Sara Prakset, who was a guest on our ship." Sara gave a small wave but did not say anything. "She's been unusually quiet," Alsoi continued, "most likely still suffering from the injuries your people were able to correct. We all thank you for helping Sara.

"Jack Arlow, Ship's Engineer, is standing next to me." Jack nodded. "And finally," Alsoi said, "Spacer First Class Jerimiah Johnson, WHOM I HAVE BEEN TRYING TO GET TO SHOW PROPER ETIQUETTE BY STANDING UP."

Jerry's face went red as he stood. "I'm sorry, Lieutenant. Ma'am, I'd like to apologize, it's all been ..."

"No need, Mr. Johnson," Ms. Sharpe interrupted. "We're a small community and remain informal so if you'd allow me to call you Jerimiah then I'd love for you to call me Hailey."

"Thank you, Hailey. My friends call me Jerry. Please do."

The lieutenant motioned for Jerry to be quiet and turned to their new host. "You're obviously a person of authority. I'd like to know why you first destroyed our ship but then go to such pains to rescue and help us. Are you part of the Mars Coalition? If so, will you allow us to return home in a prisoner exchange? I'm sure you can bargain quite handsomely for the freedom of our journalist. She's well known if you haven't already heard of her."

Hailey let out a small laugh. "Mr. Alsoi, did you see us attack you? Of course not. Not even though your captain chose to fire on us not once, but two times. It was your captain's decision to follow us into the Tippler Cylinder. Despite this, you are here alive and well solely because of our good intentions.

"As I said, I regret what happened to your shipmates but we are not part of your conflict with the colonists on Mars and Venus. You are not prisoners and if you agree to not cause mischief and to stay away from any areas we designate as 'off limits' then you may have free roam of our ship, except for a few areas that could prove harmful to you.

"As for a prisoner exchange, there are some things you must first see before we discuss such actions. Let me assure you, we fully intend to return you to Earth, but more on this later."

Hailey gave Alsoi a warm smile as a chime filled the cabin. "Watch outside now. The captain will alter course any second."

The only sign of their ship changing course was when the spinning strings swung off to the side. This was no surprise to Lt. Alsoi. Wavedrive vessels used a reactionless drive. Its field inundated and surrounded everything within it, activating every sub-electron particle to higher energy states that allowed the electron's bound graviton sub-particles to link to gravitonic radiation, the waves of gravity that saturate the universe. Since the field carried every sub-electron particle of cargo, ship and its personnel like a surfboard rider, passengers and cargo never felt a jolt or acceleration. The relativistic limits of infinite mass-change and lightspeed barriers inherent to Einsteinian Physics no longer mattered.

Details in the tunnel wall clarified with their approach. They were drawing near, heading for what appeared to be a knot of clouds laced with flashes of savage energy. Alsoi asked, "I thought we turned away from the glowing strings. There's a bundle of them over there leading into that maelstrom, same spot we're heading for."

Alsoi glanced over at Hailey and thought he saw something tiny disappear from her shoulder, then decided he was seeing things.

Hailey replied, "You've good eyes, Lieutenant. That's a kink in the string and, because of it, we have an exit portal from the Tippler Cylinder. The passage will be turbulent but we've little choice. There are only a few exit points. Now, hang on to something."

A new chime sounded, and they hit the storm wall. The ship jolted twice and shuttered. Alsoi was about to comment that he'd never felt a wavedrive powered ship react to anything, but the view outside stopped the words from ever forming.

They were outside, once again in the hard vacuum of space. The tumultuous bands of the great gas planet were to starboard, but there the resemblance to their familiar universe ended.

A set of rings, rivaling even those of Saturn, arched above them until they disappeared behind the far horizon. Eclipsing even the grandeur of the rings was an immense star-studded dome. Several moons, all of them much too close to the mother planet to survive, glowed brightly in their reflection of the distant Sun. But the immensity of the distant starfield shamed all.

Billions of stars set in a velvet black vault surrounded them in a contrast that can only exist in the vacuum of space. Stars spread across a great streak of space that was wider than the familiar Milky Way. A decade of life in space had not prepared Alsoi for such a spectral display, an expanse so grand he felt an urge to squint and protect his eyes.

Hailey simply smiled as she sipped her tea. Alsoi wondered if she had been here many times before, and had witnessed even grander displays.

***

It screamed directly into Lt. Alsoi's psyche, a directive commanding him to attend his battle station. To his surprise, he found he knew where to go. It felt like he'd always known just where his station was and how to get there.

The others must have also received a call, they were up, standing, sending questioning looks over to the lieutenant. Pale-faced and shaking, Sara blurted out, "Why do they want us to arm ourselves and await orders? How do I arm myself? How did they get inside my brain?"

Alsoi was already on his way out the door. "Not sure what's going on, but I've been ordered elsewhere. We've no choice. Comply with your command."

The passage was strangely empty as he quick-stepped down a familiar section, then turned into a completely new area of their ship. The information he needed was always there in his mind, as though he'd been this way a thousand times. He knew this was the right way. He knew how to get there but he had no concept of what waited ahead. It was then he realized that the deck was speeding him along, accelerating as he moved, pushing him forward at a speed that doubled his quick-pace step. Without warning, the glideway abruptly dropped him into the deck. There was no feeling of falling. His pace continued uninterrupted, but his heart nearly stopped with the vision presented. As though in a vid, he passed through decking that had no more substance than a cloud. But its surface flashed by like a swimmer jumping feet first into the ocean. A quick, blurred vision of the darkened plastisteel innards of the deck raced by and he was descending from the overhead of the passageway that had been below. Never slowing, that deck also careened past. Then again and again and again. He lost count by the time his downward descent ended and the only sensory confirmation that he had reached his destination was visual. He followed a passageway through a portal in the bulkhead that opened as he approached and entered a huge hangar. An officer standing in the distance was his obvious destination. Many crewmembers were already there but others arrived after him, magically materializing through the hangar bulkhead, deck and overhead with no more obvious resistance than if they had just passed through a vid image.

"Where's yer sidearm, mister?" A stocky man in what Alsoi now recognized as a naval officer's uniform addressed him. "You're outta uniform, Lieutenant. Ah, shoot. So, you're Lieutenant Alsoi? She sez you're flight qualified, that's why the call-up reached you. Well, you're not fighter qualified with our technology so direct yourself over to Commander Pearson's flight. I'm moving you from fighter pilot to a navigator's support position on a Wraith Gunship. They'll give you the basics and show you how to brane-skip. There's nothing like learning on the job. Move it. They're outbound in a minute."

Alsoi somehow recognized Commander Pearson who, without a spoken word, directed him over to three others standing next to a bulkhead. They turned as he approached.

"You haven't had time to grow proficient in hive communications so let me introduce myself. I'm Commander Markly. Stand here in column directly behind the others. You will be last to load. Just keep your arms and elbows tucked in."

Markly briefed him rapidly as he positioned the lieutenant at the aft end of the group. "We are here to stop a brane breech. On this one, you're along for the ride. Don't touch anything, even if you feel like you understand the ship. You don't. All you can do is watch and learn. Do anything more and you'll get us killed.

"Now stand. Our gunship will be forming in a moment. There behind Yohanson and to the left. Good enough. It's a bit unnerving the first time but don't worry, the Wraith birth will take care of everything. See, it's already started."

Alsoi became aware of a countdown sequence. It was more like a bit of an afterthought or memory rather than something he was concentrating on. He grew tense as the countdown neared its end.

The usual black haze formed in front of the group, thickening as it rolled toward them. Alsoi chuckled to no one in particular. *Every damn thing with these people starts with black smoke. Nothing is solid. What the hell is this universe coming to?*

To his astonishment, he found he knew the answer. It wasn't smoke at all. They were NullBots, autonomous, programmed robots whose name derived from the nullification of electron sub-particle bonds to release gravitons that were the basic constituent of each NullBot, constructs of pure energy bosons rather than the fermion base of matter familiar to humans in the form of electrons, atoms, and all the material elements.

NullBots were so small that when millions of them clustered together, they became nothing more than a tiny particle of smoke. Smoke particles whose capabilities and intelligence increased as more and more individuals clustered until the smoke became a dense cloud capable of stopping even the passage of energetic photons.

The NullBots were programmable as individuals or as a unified swarm. And as the cloud grew denser, the swarm's intelligence increased, until it became solid enough to function as a semi-intelligent drone, or eventually, an autonomous entity that could achieve a state of self-awareness, capable of learning, self-programming, and replication – sentience.

The haze morphed into a shiny, solid black wall just before it reached the pilot and copilot standing at attention two rows before Alsoi. Rainbow colored lines thrashed across the black surface as it steadily glided toward them. No one stepped back or flinched, but stood firm in its path. Alsoi clenched his jaw and promised himself he wouldn't budge a muscle.

The wall flowed over and around the first two. They disappeared like figurines dipped into a bowl of thick black lava. They were gone and he was next. Alsoi didn't move but he couldn't help but close his eyes and only opened them when he sensed the commander communicating. "Hey Newbie, wakey wakey. You managed to survive."

Years had passed since anyone last called him 'Newbie,' but there was no malice in the commander's calls. Alsoi's eyes snapped open. "Christ on a toadstool, we're in a boat."

"She's not a 'boat,' Newbie. You're in the deadliest vessel know to humanity, a Wraith Gunship. Crewed by four, with elbowroom to squeeze in excess baggage. That's you, in case you're wondering. Now sit back, watch and learn. No questions. If you want to know something, ask your Hive. We'll jaw about it later. If we survive."

Alsoi was about to ask what his 'Hive' was when he noticed he was no longer standing but seated. That is, he was in a seated position. He could feel something beneath him but physically, there was nothing. They were in an egg-shaped, light-grey cabin, suspended mid-center of an oblate spheroid just large enough to hold them in the same relative positions with pilot and copilot up front. Controls flashed into existence beneath the pilot's hands then disappeared as the adjustment completed. The middle two crew members were busy staring off in the distance. Alsoi wondered why, and it came to him they were calibrating a weapons system, reconfiguring it.

Markley turned back to check his crew and announced, "Heads up. We're next."

The walls of their Wraith disappeared. Alsoi had a moment's glimpse of the hangar filled with shining black eggs and then they were gone, replaced by a spectacular panorama of stars and a Milky Way that was much too bright as it streaked across the sky beneath their feet. Jupiter and its strange rings were gone, and a portion of the port-side view was nothing but a black hole in the starfield.

"That's *Athos*, our mother ship," said a male voice Alsoi did not recognize. "She's absorbing photons and any other radiation that impacts her, stealth mode standard combat status.

"I'm Thompson, the navigator. You're to learn from me so pay attention."

The stars began jittering, vibrating ever so slightly, and the black 'hole' in space that was their mothership rapidly shrunk in size until it disappeared completely. A visual plot popped into Alsoi's brain, accompanied by Thompson's voice. "That's our course. Our destination is the far edge of the Oort Cloud, roughly thirty-seven point five degrees above the ecliptic. You can plot course alternatives using your navigator's app, directions will come to you as you use it. If you run into problems, ask our gunship. She answers to 'Matilda.'

"Our objective's a bit more than a lightyear out, gathering high atomic weight elements from the comets in the jetsam of the cloud. They're preparing for a strike. Not sure what they're gonna try this time. It's always a little different. Our job is to make sure they don't get lucky and succeed.

"Gonna take us an hour to get there so you have time to meet Matilda and learn how to be a Nav-Assistant. Yeah, you heard right, an hour. Normally it would take longer to get out there because of the high in-system gravitic wave-chop from all the planets, but there's a relatively smooth region where Jupiter's huge gravitational field swamps the gravitic waves from all the other sources in the solar system. This is a region with smooth sailing and we'll use it to accelerate as we climb up and above the ecliptic of the solar system where it's still a bit bumpy. But we'll be able to accelerate to '9c,' or nine times lightspeed. Our target's only moving at roughly 0.3c as their ram-scoop gathers jetsam, so it's a good time to hit them. As we enter striking distance, we'll luff the wavefront and hit them at near zero relative velocity. With any luck they won't be expecting us.

"Any questions, ask Matilda. She's a new ship but don't worry about her short AI Training cycle. Wraith ships don't go through lengthy programming since we learned how to store ship's personality between instances of their materialization. Oh shit, you didn't follow that, did you? *Athos*, our mothership, said you were behind technically. It's not a problem, Matilda will bring you up to speed."

The voice and image of a pleasant and very athletic young lady came to Alsoi. "Good morning, Lieutenant. I'm the avatar for Matilda and I'm very anxious to help you get up to speed."

Alsoi realized he was a slow learner. Matilda tried, but failed several times to dump the lessons into his brain. His background was simply too primitive for a straight data dump. Eventually, she zeroed in on a threshold that, with a little pain, she could convey concepts simple enough for him to understand.

He learned about the drones they manufactured called NullBots, solid creatures composed of boson energy bundles rather than the fermion-base elements that made up his familiar universe. The NullBot individuals were small enough that their passing through an atom was less difficult than a ship crossing the empty space between planets of the solar system. Like the enormous release of energy when the bonds of an atom split, NullBot bosons emerged with an even greater energy release when an electron split into its graviton sub-particles—gravitons, the dark matter particle equivalent of the gravity waves that formed the basis of the universe and traveled through it at hundreds, even thousands of times the speed of the energy that humans call light particles or photons.

Alsoi was surprised to learn his body already harbored colonies of NullBots from the seeds first planted when Gunny Arlington infected them with the black haze during the shuttle rescue. It was then the NullBots first replicated inside of him and began cruising through his body. When they encountered defects, the NullBots repaired or eliminated them. They destroyed harmful aliens to the body, such as predatory bacteria and viruses, by breaking them down to their sub-electron particles and creating new NullBots. They repaired any genetic defects of his DNA. The lieutenant was now part of a network of instant gravitic communications between those traveling on the *Athos* and its AI centers. Faster-than-light Hive Communication's links for data storage as well as the sharing of information and commands, all instantly transported directly to the visual, conceptual and storage areas of his brain.

Multicolored points of starlight performed their jittery dance as Matilda and forty-seven other Wraith Gunships and Foxfire Fighters sped outward, rising high above the ecliptic of the solar system and outward until Sol was little more than a bright point in the heavens. Then they readjusted their gravity-links and luffed inward, dumping velocity for a rendezvous with the invader.

***

Alsoi's head ached from the force-fed information dump. Stretching stiffened muscles, his tired eyes relaxed by looking out into the infinite expanse of the universe that began just outside the protective, but strangely pliant, invisible walls of their gunship less than an arm's length away. The others were busy. For now, his job was to watch and learn. Boring. His eyes strained to see if anything outside had changed. They widened in surprise as they registered on an obviously immense object, lying dead ahead on their course.

If this really is our solar system, then why have I never seen or heard of anything like this? he thought. *Even at this distance, we would have sensed an obvious breach in the fabric of our universe as dramatic as this.*

What appeared at first to be a jagged rent in the fabric of the universe ran across the heavens ahead. It was a window and through it peeked a wall of blazing hot stars and gas. It all shined with a brilliance dimming even the splendor he'd first seen on their exit from the Red Spot of Jupiter, just a few scant hours earlier. The materials he'd just absorbed allowed him to speculate on the phenomenon.

I thought this was all theoretical but there it is. A rough window or more like a tear in the fabric of space, perhaps a cosmic string ripped open, revealing another dimension. No, that's not right, Matilda calls it a 'brane.' I guess 'dimension' is close enough. The paper said that a few years ago such things were only a concept, an artifact of string theory physics. Yet here one is and we're heading right for it. What could possibly be on the other side of that jagged tear? Is it a window into the heart of a star cluster or perhaps the center of our galaxy?

Visuals and broadband frequency analysis of data gathered by millions of autonomous sub-microscopic drones scouting ahead of the strike force and enhanced by Matilda combined into a targeting display that solidified before him. Highlighted near the edge of the jagged rip was their target. It was another great ship or perhaps an animal. A shapeshifting, obviously alien and rather repulsive dull-black form constantly churning as it moved forward, flinging out long tendrils across the heavens ahead of it with the curling, groping motion of an octopus clawing its way across some nonexistent seafloor. A huge, churning sphere of pure energy followed behind the alien ship, planting in Alsoi's mind the vision of a spider on a web dragging its mummified prey behind.

Matilda's contact broke his fascination. "You are correct, the thing it drags is an energy bundle. Similar past encounters suggest it is creating the bundle from local debris it converts into pure energy but how they intend to use it we have no idea. This is something new. We don't know how they will employ this, but probability-based analysis of past encounters suggests they will use it as a weapon against us. They move fast and our attack group from the *Athos* is the only asset we have in striking distance. It was pure chance that our encounter with your ship forced us to return as soon as we did. There will be no second chance. Pay attention now. The fighter wing is about to go in."

Single pilot Foxfire Fighters led the initial wave. They sailed in hot and heavy, leaving ion trails in their wake that fluoresced in the deep purple of high-frequency energy as they tacked across gravity wavefronts, dumping both speed and energy in a swooping direct assault of the alien mothership. No enemy fighters rose to meet them. Instead, flickering strings of light whipped out from the alien, streaking far into space before their tips sheared and went spinning onward like a boomerang of pure lightning launched toward their target. The fighters replied defensively with staccato bursts of photon bolts that flew across the gap like strings of fiery pearls, discharging and releasing the energy of the alien whip in fantastic bursts of visible light and gamma rays that appeared on the enhanced displays of Matilda, surrounded by flashing aurora borealis bands of released deadly energy.

A mind-numbing flash darkened Matilda's displays. They quickly recovered. Ahead and to the side of their trajectory was a wickedly throbbing hotspot that persisted as its energy wave washed over them. Pure energy released from the ripping of atomic bonds and dark matter that sailed out across the void, washing over Matilda in a chaos-driven tsunami her sensors interpreted as a screeching wail. The stars returned along with a nebula of glowing particles where three of the Foxfires existed moments before.

"Ah, poor Jimmy. Caught in the energy burst of ..." The copilot began under his breath before the pilot's reprimand descended upon him.

"Stay focused, we're up next."

Their viewpoint shifted as the Wraith swung around, avoiding the worst of the plasma's hot energy particle cloud. Alsoi watched the navigator plot an impossible course that jigged across the intervening void, narrowly avoiding the attack patterns laid out by other Wraiths sailing in from all directions, every one of them hoping the fighters managed to clear their path to the target ahead.

"Drones armed and primed." The steady voice of the weapons officer sounded off in their minds. The cabin around them wailed under the onslaught of high energy particles and stress.

Alsoi queried Matilda's status. Its reply instantly returned, "I am preparing antimatter weapons systems composed of drones, essentially dumb NullBot entities capable of only the most basic programming. They form energy packets, basically armed torpedoes that attack by turning on each drone's replication cycle. The weapon's master will arm and release them after laying in the signature of the target."

The bombardier released the antimatter drone torpedoes. One by one they came to life, instantly identifying their target. High energy drives linked to the crests of the local graviton waves and the torpedoes left, streaking out across the heavens in less than three milliseconds. Upon entering sensor range of the first sizeable chunk of matter or antimatter matching the profile of their target, the drone torpedoes fragmented, releasing billions of tiny, dumb NullBots programmed only for one task. They ripped into the atom-matrix of anything they contacted, tearing at it on a sub-atomic scale by shredding its atomic bonds and ferociously cracking even their target's electron shells, releasing deadly bursts of protons, antimatter, and gravitons that instantly rephased into new, weaponized NullBots. NullBots that reformed, continuing onward to repeat the reproductive expansion until they consumed the entire target.

Atomic fires flared across the Oort Cloud from successful strikes. The surviving Wraiths jigged and swooped inward, pressing their attack as the alien vessel lashed out in defense and put up energy screens before their drone torpedoes. When a torpedo struck the alien energy screen, a blast followed as it converted torpedoes into incoherent waves of dirty energy. Its defenses were massive, but the alien was taking damage. Still, it suffered little compared to the losses inflicted upon its attackers as Wraith after Wraith flashed into pure energy, leaving behind only clouds of angry radiation that sublimated into nonexistence nearly as rapidly as they formed.

A tsunami of chaos and helplessness washed over Alsoi. Greater than any fear of death, he screamed in frustration. They were losing and all he could do was sit and watch.

Commander Markley's rocksteady command voice managed to cut through the chaos. He called out to the last four surviving Wraiths of his flight. "We're the last hope, forget the safeties and take your loads in to point blank."

Blue fire materialized as a searing lens of energy in the cabin next to Alsoi. It immediately sent a blinding flash across the cabin that cut into the commander and his copilot, instantly converting them to vapor and ionized gas. Alsoi sensed his NullBots clamp his air intake. They began creating oxygen within his body, using matter conversion, pumping the lifegiving gas directly into his bloodstream to replace the function of his airless lungs. The lieutenant's attention never veered from the deadly lens of fire filling the cabin, so close to him he could sense its evil intent.

In the eternity that passed in less than a heartbeat, the blue fire directed a second blast of energy at the navigator and bombardier seated in the second row. Everything inside the gunship was breaking apart or vaporizing, including the two officers who flashed into an expanding vapor cloud as rapidly as the pilots. Alsoi fell back in fear, slipping on a sidearm that had landed beneath his foot. He tumbled to the deck, fighting the blazing grip of an alien mind clamping around his consciousness. His hand gripped the weapon. He'd never fired one, but pistol designs were optimized for the human hand, and his fingers folded by instinct around the grip. He brought the weapon up and fired. The blast broke the searing grip warping his consciousness. Better aimed, his second load struck the ethereal lens dead center. Quite unexpectedly, the thing shrieked, its squeal played across Alsoi's nervous system, ripping sensitive nerves like the amplified screech of fingernails scraping across a chalkboard.

Then, it was gone.

Battered, shaking, and mind numb, Alsoi knew if he stopped he would never move again. He crawled forward through a cabin filled with the aerated mush of dead NullBots, body parts, and vapor-converted human remains, pulling himself to the front of the Wraith. Matilda was barely responding. She was sluggish but seemed to be slowly shaking off the effects of the attack. Self-repair was underway. For the first time, Alsoi linked directly to the gunship, his mind ripped through systems he didn't understand and past those too badly damaged to be recognizable. His understanding of the ship grew as he grasped mentally at its controls and found what he was looking for. Weapon's control was operational, but the raw dark matter reservoir used for the antimatter torpedoes was gone.

The concept rammed into his brain like a weapon system charging. Matilda was coming around and the words clashed in his mind. "Use the remains strewn across the cabin. Help me direct the weapon charging sequence."

Weak as she was, he still recognized her voice. Alsoi concentrated, directing the free-radical NullBots spread across the cabin to gather the atomized remains. Then he used the command channel to search out the universe around him. They were spinning out of control, but on a course that would graze the alien. He plotted a firing point without regard for safe-distance, completely disregarding weapon's release protocols. The ship yielded, firing to him as it focused its few remaining resources to reshape a damaged antimatter torpedo into a crude NullBot energy casing.

Alsoi didn't wait for the 'ready' signal from the ship but fired as they came to bear. The torpedo ripped out across a section of space with a ferocity that would have made a stellar furnace blanch and released its load before the casing could complete sublimation into pure energy.

Its load of NullBots matured in the billionth of a second it took to reach their target. Already high in the energetic phase of their reproductive cycle, they ripped into the alien, splitting its sub-atomic particles, converting them into antimatter. The process released waves of energy that regrouped into gravitic particles pre-programmed to create new, highly active deadly NullBots.

The skies experienced no dramatic blast of released energy. The alien simply disappeared, consumed in its entirety. As it died, the window to another brane of the universe closed, leaving one Wraith Gunship and three Foxfire Fighters alone in the familiar starfield of their universe.

***

"If I were to label you a survivor, Lieutenant," said a man's voice. "I would place myself in danger of being ridiculed by others for extreme understatement."

Invasive. Unwanted. Undeniable. Each word slammed into Alsoi, clattering through his mind with a life of its own.

The first challenge was for him to open his eyes. It was hard. He couldn't. Pain racked his body, emanating from each muscle. He couldn't feel anything beyond the agony. No sensory input. Nothing.

More words slashed across his psyche. He ignored them in his growing panic and willed his eyes to open.

Nothing. Can't see a thing. Wait. No, not right. Hallucination? White filaments of mist bending, twisting. Can I move my arm?

The cloaking mist slowly cleared and something shiny flickered. Alsoi strained to move his arm.

"One more minute, Lieutenant. Everything's fine." The voice was a woman's this time, soothing and oh so clear. His world shuddered. He tried moving but couldn't. The woman's voice came back. "Patience, everything is okay. I'm going to cancel the field and you're going to feel weight and then some pressure on your back. It's okay, we moved you to a bed. You are safe and I'm going to cut the field in 3… 2…1."

He was falling. He shut his eyes, but the sensation had already passed. Somehow, he sensed a bed and clean sheets. He chanced to open his eyes and saw a man hovering over him.

"Lieutenant, you back with us, boy?"

Yes. Yes, I am and … I don't know you. You wear a captain's bars but …

"Lieutenant, you have to speak out loud. Use your lips. Come on, it shouldn't be this hard. Buckle up, lad, and gather …"

"What? Wha … Who are you? Where am I? Ugh, I'm sorry, sir … Captain that is. I just …"

"That's more like it and I'm not a captain or even an officer. I work for a living and right now you are my biggest problem and that's not a good thing to be." The man turned a brief, angry glance to someone out of Alsoi's sight.

"I wanted to be the first one you saw when you wakened. I can't imagine how you could not remember my handsome face and sparkling disposition. Gunny Arlington, your ex-babysitter and still a gunnery sergeant by the skin of my teeth after Captain Arlonious Tafton chewed me out.

"What kind of a gung-ho Joe are you anyway? I give you guys a little freedom and you go running off with a flight squadron and end up getting people killed. I should … What?"

The flight nurse was tapping the bar on her shoulder. "See that bar, Sergeant? I think it's time for you to leave. I told you not to upset my patient. Not another word. Out."

The nurse returned her attention to the patient. "I apologize, Lieutenant Alsoi. That was not supposed to happen."

Alsoi was too tired to move his head and follow the sergeant's departure. A familiar face came into view, Doctor Metrix. As usual, he was babbling about something. "You should expect to feel lethargic and confused. Your cycle was interrupted. You're going back into regeneration. I apologize for waking you, but the sergeant said it was important. Now sleep. You'll feel much better afterward. One good thought, I'm sure you'll be relieved to know we're almost home."

***

The room came to life with the entry of Captain Arlonious Tafton. Three HiveBot drones, little larger than a fly themselves and quite different from the NullBots, buzzed by his head on a direct path for an honest-to-goodness insect that had somehow managed to survive inside his office. The chase stole the captain's attention for a moment, the insect fought hard, but the end was inevitable. Just a bug that was now gone but even so, he admired anything that showed a determination to survive and stay the course.

Three officers and Gunny entered from the opposite side of the oval chamber. The chamber's bulkheads and overhead displayed a complete panorama of the star-studded universe, as though the officers were assembling around a conference table located on the outer skin of the vessel.

"Be seated." The captain didn't bother to look up at the others as he took a pen from his pocket and set it on the table. It glowed, stood on end and the necessary procedural guide, as well as the captain's own notes, appeared, perfectly arrayed on the surface before him.

"We are here convened to initiate proceedings against Nichols Alsoi, former Lieutenant of the International Space Agency, Earth. Bring in the defendant."

A passage opened on the opposing side of the room and two Spacer Ratings led Alsoi in.

"Let him sit, he's still recovering," said the captain.

"No, sir," Alsoi protested, "if I'm to be tried under court-martial, I will stand …"

"Don't be ridiculous, Lieutenant. You've just emerged from a medical tank. Sit. It is necessary you be of clear mind so that you understand the severity of your actions and the resulting charges.

"Nichols Alsoi, ISA Lieutenant," the captain said, beginning the proceedings, "you are charged with entering a restricted action area, boarding a CS vessel illegally and causing the death of said vessel's crew. How do you plead?"

"Not guilty, sir," Alsoi said. "And I object. This court does not have legal jurisdiction over me."

"Be it entered in the record that a 'not guilty' plea has been submitted. The court recognizes the defendant's objection of non-jurisdiction and declares the objection overruled since the defendant is no longer in ISA legal jurisdiction but is a guest of the CS.

"Lieutenant Alsoi, to your right is Commander Alcaise Brown. She is your legal counsel.

"Lieutenant Jonah Rogers is acting prosecutor. For the record, please repeat the case against Lt. Alsoi."

The prosecutor began. "Lieutenant Nichols Alsoi did enter a fleet restricted area under false authorization where he was assigned to Wraith Gunship Matilda as a navigational observer. The gunship's mission in attack wing three was to locate a brane intrusion and destroy all enemy craft before they could assemble for launch. The wing located the intrusion and with Foxfire Fighters flying cover, initiated their attack. Upon the commencement of the action, brane warriors boarded their gunship. Lieutenant Alsoi managed to obtain possession of a sidearm without authorization. The crew perished but not before they selflessly destroyed the enemy vessel in heroic action.

"The Wraith Gunship carrying Mr. Alsoi was disabled but later discovered in a sweep of the sector with two survivors rescued. It was then revealed that the weapon held by Alsoi had been discharged a total of four bursts, thereby initiating the submission of charges."

"Lieutenant Alsoi," said the captain, "have you anything to add to this description?"

Alsoi did not respond.

"Lieutenant, I will not repeat myself. You are ordered to remain seated. Do so."

"I'm sorry, sir," Alsoi said. "The exact circumstances of the encounter are not entirely clear, but I recall things a little differently."

Alsoi reviewed his mission from memory. He found he could recall an amazing amount of detail but there were still unclear areas, particularly around the incident where he found the weapon and discharged it.

"Sir, I wish to emphasize that I was in fear for my life. I had no knowledge of what that lenticular blaze of energy was. I only knew it was responsible for the deaths of my shipmates. My discharges went to that strange apparition. After that, the torpedo run and release were all instinct. I was having difficulty breathing and didn't consider what occurred in my surroundings, much less how I knew what to do."

"Thank you, Lieutenant."

"The court recognizes Commander Brown."

"Thank you, sir," said Commander Brown. "I've received notification that the other survivor has completed second plateau regeneration and is now capable of testifying. I would like to bring it into chambers to offer testimony."

"Do so, Commander," said the captain.

The wall again opened for the entry of a comely Lieutenant.

"State your name, rank and function for the record. Then please be seated."

"Lieutenant Matilda, cs708861. My function is Wraith Gunship, but I'm currently installed in this frame because of limitations imposed upon entering second plateau regeneration."

The captain nodded. "Log into court records that Lieutenant Matilda is temporarily assuming the form of a female second lieutenant in appropriate uniform and in accordance with its rank.

"Lieutenant Matilda. Your NullBot mass is considerably reduced in this configuration. Please validate the accuracy of your memory of the incident and intellect logic level."

"Sir, archived and active memory storage is ninety-eight point three one seven accurate to a six-sigma probability estimate. Intellect is sixty-seven point two one Kessler, the majority of loss is incurred within Wraith operations and navigation. That is an area not needed until I reform in Wraith containment."

"Approved," said the captain. "You may proceed as a valid participant and expert witness. Please summarize the timeframe from the initiation of your weapons delivery run."

"Yes, sir. I reviewed the testimony given by the defendant and agree but for the following exceptions.

"My attack initiated at eighteen hundred forty-seven hours point five hours. Three Foxfires led the way and the Wraith Squadron was in the final stage of a Lissajous IV Defensive Weave attack pattern. Lieutenant Alsoi's station was located at the rear of the cockpit. Weapons were arming when a brane warrior boarded, immediately discharging lethal fire by first targeting the pilot and copilot. The alien directed a second salvo at navigation and the weapons officers. All four crewmembers ceased life function despite extensive rejuvenation attempts by their NullBot nervous system components.

"The lieutenant's NullBot interface was in its growth and adaptation stage, as it is now. Despite this impediment, he sensed a personal handgun underfoot that had ejected from the navigator's holster and recognized its function. His reaction was swift and correct as he discharged four bursts at the brane boarding party.

"Lieutenant Alsoi's aim was true and the threat was eliminated. But the cabin was filling with a mixture of hydrocarbons, carbon monoxide, and halogen gas. Despite being in the process of succumbing to these gases, Lieutenant Alsoi managed to initiate a link to weapons and force a release of the fully armed torpedo spread before Wraith targeting could fully recover.

"Lieutenant Alsoi's instinct was off in its targeting by sixty-two thousandths of a second but was sufficient to affect a hit on the brane vessel. The vessel was completely destroyed. So our mission's secondary objective to obtain samples and lifeforms were not accomplished. But the primary goal of stopping the attack and sealing the breach was met."

"Lieutenant Matilda," said the captain, "please explain why you chose to reveal weapons discharge methods to an outsider."

"Lieutenant Alsoi had, and retains, full clearance that was issued upon ship's system recognition of his pilot qualifications, emergency directive AL32.322 covering a category one brane breach. His actions were legal, authorized by central programming and responsible for the success of the mission."

Captain Tafton sat back and looked up into the stars for a few moments before turning to the prosecutor. "Have you any rebuttal or commentary?"

"In view of this testimony, prosecution withdraws all charges."

"Then court-martial is adjourned," said the captain. "Gunnery Staff Sergeant Arlington, you will accompany Lieutenant Nichols Alsoi back to his quarters. He will receive notification of his next assignment at the appropriate time. Be aware that Ship's AI has accepted his induction into the CS Fleet and he is officially an officer and a gentleman by act and actions. Congratulations, Lieutenant Alsoi.

"Gunny, you and the Lieutenant will remain. The rest of you are dismissed."

As chambers cleared, Captain Arlonious Tafton stood and crossed over to the bulkhead. It opened as he approached. Alsoi was amazed to see an old-fashioned drink dispenser and a glass drinking service. "You're surprised?" The captain laughed. "It's one of my few personal vices, Lieutenant.

The captain glanced at the gunny. "You too, Trent? The usual?"

The gunny laughed. "You're suddenly informal, Arlonious."

"It's not every day that someone achieves first entry as a full Lieutenant into the CS. What'll it be, and may I call you Nichols?"

"I'd be honored, sir," said Alsoi, "but I'm also a bit confused. Hey, you guessed right. I haven't had a single malt in months. Thank you.

"I never expressed a desire to join you and I haven't been sworn in. What right have you to shanghai me?"

"You will not be brought into service against your will," said the captain. "And until you are voluntarily sworn in, you cannot issue binding orders. This induction is an honor extended to you by me and that of *Athos*, our ship. And it's underwritten by Gunship Matilda. Your actions prove your worth and I'd certainly like to be your sponsor, should you accept induction."

"Thank you, but I already have a valid oath of allegiance to the ISA."

"Lieutenant, that oath is no longer valid. The ISA does not, and has never existed in this universe."

"I don't understand." Alsoi furrowed his brow. "How can you say it has never existed?"

"We're not at liberty to disclose that information and neither is gunny," replied the captain, "so don't attempt to trick the answers from him. These things you must discover on your own, or else you will never truly believe. But don't worry, discover them you will.

"Now, we all have other duties. Thank you, gentlemen. You are dismissed."

✳✳✳

"I'll be back."

GySgt. Trent Arlington was in a vile, dark mood ever since the captain chewed him out for berating Alsoi in medical, and he was doing the most natural, most logical thing to remedy the situation. He was taking it out on

Corporal Prachert. "You sit with the young'ins and keep an eye on 'em until I return."

"One of these days, Alice," Jack Arlow whined under his breath as the GySgt. left. "One of these days. Pow, to da moon."

Corporal Prachert turned a puzzled looked at Arlow.

Arlow's comment didn't faze Spacer Jerry Johnson. He'd known and worked with the engineer for years. He knew Jack could never keep his mouth shut. "Arlow, you are the weirdest engineer I've never met and yes Ms. Prakset, I did say 'never' so don't go pushin' none of your grammar Nazi tactics on me. Don't know what you're griping about. It ain't that bad. We're back in the lounge.

"Well, except for the lieutenant.

"This is rather awkward, Corporal, would you mind if I call you Molly? Prachert and Prakset are just too close for me to keep track of.

She rolled her eyes.

"Look, you can tell us, is Alsoi dead? What happened?"

Molly Prakset sighed. "Can't say a word, Jerry. Let's change the subject, okay?"

People passed by and were friendly, but none stopped to strike up a conversation, although some stared at them longingly, obviously wanting to speak with them. Everyone apparently knew the survivors by name, but when asked, refused to answer questions about their lieutenant, where this strange ship came from, what would happen to them or where in the universe they might be. They all received the same answer. 'Wait until we're home.' When asked how long that would be, the answer was 'a few hours.'

Sara Prakset, ever the practical journalist, broke the short silence that followed. "Now you know how I feel. I'm way behind all of you on current events because of my leg injury. I've obviously missed a lot. Could we all just sit a little while and bring me up to date on what's happening?

"One minute though, I'm not doing this dry. Hey, hey, you. We'd like to order." She waved to a waiter who immediately came over. *That's odd, I don't have to ask for a menu, I already know what's available. Fantastic, I haven't had one of these in years and …* "Hey, you're already writing down my order?"

The waiter stopped, looking a bit shocked. "Oh, I'm sorry. Would you rather I wait before writing your order or perhaps I should not input it to the tablet at all?"

"No, no. That's all right, I guess it's just that … How is it you know what I'm ordering before even I do?"

"You told me, ma'am. You desired several items but decided on this one red wine mixer. An excellent choice if I say so."

"Neat trick. Say, where are you from anyway?"

"I'm from the Station, of course."

"No. Where were you born? Where'd ya grow up?"

"Oh, I apologize if I gave you the wrong impression. You could have downloaded my registry at … oh dear. You don't know, do you?"

Sara's blank look said it all.

"I'm a synthetic, ma'am. A bot, if you wish to use the vernacular. Properly designated. I'm a third generation NullBot Hive Entity. I currently serve as luxury support for the lounge, but I can do many things, including critical care and programming for alternative hive interfaces. I do like to change regularly. Keeps me from getting bored. Now, if there are no more questions, I'll retrieve your orders … ugh, unless your friends would also prefer to vocalize them to me. No? Thank you."

They spent the next hour bringing Sara up to date, interrupted many times by her questions and the waiter magically bringing over additional refreshments whenever they seemed to get the craving. Sara was feeling loose, a bit tipsy, but never bad enough to lose control or stagger. Eventually, the tension of all they'd been through began to surface.

"We're in a bad situation," said Sara, "and I feel a little guilty."

Jerry's gaze went to the surrounding starfield panorama. "That's a normal reaction but you shouldn't feel guilty because you survived. Remember, we ain't outta this yet. We don't know how we're gonna get home or what they intend doing with us."

Corporal Prachert, ever in control of the situation, sat forward. "You've been pretty damn lucky. Want to know where you are? You're alive. You survived. Sara's broken leg would have been fatal in any other disaster situation back from where you came. Instead she's up and walking around as though the injury never occurred.

"You should be feeling pretty good. You've been treated with courtesy and respect."

Jerry plopped back onto the cushion and let out a loud grunt. "That's because they know we can't do nothing about it. We're screwed."

The corporal replied, "Bull, there's always something you can do, but if you're planning anything violent, forget about it. You can't win. Anyways, consider this. We would never have rescued you if we intended to harm you. We even took a risk. After we saved you, we could have simply shut you up in a cargo hold or closet to live on bread and water. Maybe even left you right where we found you. That would have prevented all your griping.

"Look, you need to play along with us a while longer until you can get in front of someone with real authority. Someone who will clearly show you what's going on from our perspective. I know none of this makes sense but give it a chance.

"Believe me. I like you and I've thought about telling you everything. The worst thing is if I were to tell you the truth right now, you wouldn't believe me. You have to see and experience a bit more."

A voice cut in. "Are you guys busy or can I join the party?"

They'd all been feeling down but recognized Alsoi's voice and nearly jumped to greet him. "They refused to tell us where you were and what happened," said Jerry. "We were thinking the worst."

"Long story," Alsoi replied, "minor problem with the captain. But we have a little time so let me bring you up to speed."

GySgt. Arlington, who had accompanied Alsoi, used the pause in conversation to speak up. "If that will be all, sir, I'll get on with my duties."

Alsoi gave Gunny a strange look, leaving Jack Arlow the opportunity to speak up first. "Whoa, major attitude shift, Gunny. Did the world just turn over? Now I'm really anxious to hear what happened."

A worried look came over the lieutenant's face, "Gunnery Staff Sergeant Arlington, for as gruff as you are, you and Corporal Prachert were our rescuers and our first friends here. I certainly hope you don't feel a need to be so formal."

"Sir, that relationship between me and the captain goes back years. I don't really know you, but the captain made very clear your contribution to the ..."

"That's not important. I'll update the others. Now, if it's possible with your duties, could you take a little time to sit down and join us for a friendly drink?"

"Yes, sir. Lieutenant."

Jerry raised his eyebrows and let out a low whistle. "Things become more and more interesting. Where should we start?"

Jack Arlow sat forward and nodded toward the star-filled panorama. "This should be a good place. Has anyone else noticed that blue star dead ahead of us is now a small blue disk?

"I suspect our destination is in sight."

***

The blue star became a disk, became a planet, and grew until they could distinguish a second silvery disk, about a quarter its diameter, next to it.

Gunny Arlington broke into their fascination. "Hailey's comin' again. Now's the time to ask questions but don't get pushy and for God's sake, don't be disrespectful. You guys are getting' the royal treatment so earn it. Hear that, Johnson?"

"Sometimes you bring back bad memories, Gunny," Jerry retorted. "Are you sure you aren't an Earthling?" Jerry's wisecracks were famous back home, but the gunny wasn't fazed.

"Never said I wasn't. Born and raised on Earth. Live there now." With that he sat down. His beer arrived but he would only smile when they asked questions about his home and the planet ahead.

Hailey arrived as they were passing by a familiar moon. Only Jack Arlow seemed to be uneasy with the satellite. He asked Hailey. "What's with Tycho?"

"I told Gunny you were sharp," she replied. "The splash rays from the crater are still relatively new and clear."

"The hell with the lunar crater," Sara interjected. "Where are we and what's that planet?"

"What's the matter, Sara?" Hailey asked.

"The planet's nothing but water and a few small islands. Something … something else isn't right. Oh, I see it now. Even with all the water, there are so few clouds and no snowcaps at the poles."

Hailey smiled. "It's so nice to have a good lead-in.

"Look. There goes our fighter escort. Nothing to concern yourself about. They're clearing a corridor ahead of us for landing."

Two small black ships went racing ahead. They entered the atmosphere much like any wavedrive vessel, performing unexpected turns, flips and even complete direction reversals, showing no concern for inertial stress or frictional heat buildup on the craft. The wavedrive's field accelerated air molecules away from the path ahead, leaving them to fly in a localized vacuum in any environment, whether it be the vacuum of space, the waters of the ocean, or the atmosphere of a planet. As they descended to the point that the curvature of the planet was about to disappear, the fighters began flying a weaving, bobbing pattern ahead of the starship's path.

"I assume the crazy antics are part of their clearing routine," said Jack, "but we're up way too high for interference. Just what is their purpose?"

Hailey's only answer was, "No, we're not too high for this planet."

They took a long, easy glide to the surface even though a direct dive would have been just as uneventful. Not even a sonic boom marred their passage, since they created no shockwave. The long glide did, however, give the fighters time to deflect several longnecked animals that were larger than the fighters, much larger if you considered their bat-like wings. They reminded Sara of brightly colored, flying giraffes with translucent batwings.

The terminator between day and night sped by as they flew over their first landmass. The night was impossibly dark, lacking even city lights to shine into the heavens. Then once again it was daylight and the craft leveled slightly in its final descent. On the horizon lay a white beach shoreline marking the separation between sea and mainland. A view of the landmass showed this to be a wild planet with jungle extending as far as the eye could see inland.

Finally, they were low enough to resolve animal life. Sara nearly shook in her fascination. "There's so much life. I've never seen …"

Hailey set down her drink and joined them. "This world is tropical, has been for hundreds of millions of years. Stable with little or no radical swings in temperature. Its subtropical climate extends as high as fifty-seven degrees above the equator. That's why there are no polar icecaps and, except for the highest peaks, no snow or ice. The world's a zoological paradise. Species are relatively stable, ever so slowly evolving for hundreds of millions of years.

"Homeport, just ahead."

A clearing in the jungle with a few buildings at its edges marked the landing pad. It lay in the foothills of mountains with a gorge and steep cliffs bordering its northern side. Inside the gorge ran a broad, strong flowing river.

Sara Prakset leaned forward to touch Hailey's arm. "It's beautiful. The entire planet's a paradise and you have the most beautiful homes, perfectly nestled in the landscape."

"Homes?" Jerry asked. "Where?"

"Silly, men," Sara replied. "They always miss the important things. Over there, Jerry. Don't look for contrasting colors and hard round edges. Look for structures the same color as their surroundings. Soft flowing designs that nestle into nature."

Alsoi replied, "Ah, I can see them now that you point them out. Many more than I would have expected.

"The military berm first caught my eye. It's that defensive earthen wall surrounding three sides of the compound. The cliffs above the river protect the fourth side. They loaded the berm with high-tech gear, most noticeably the autosentinels guard towers spaced along the top. I know military armament, but this tower design is something I've never seen before and it looks lethal.

"Judging by the design of the autosentinels, threats obviously exist on this world and they are both big and deadly. Ms. Sharpe, your paradise seems to have a very dark side to it."

GySgt. Arlington appeared. "You're gonna have plenty of time for sightseeing. I'm to take you to Captain Tafton. He'll provide the introductions and address all your concerns. Follow me."

"Us too?" Jerry asked.

"Of course, all of you, unless you want to get right to work. I can deal that out too if you want."

They entered a world of sunshine, warm temperature and humidity. In spite of the heat, Sara felt invigorated and unconsciously began pulling in great lungfuls of wonderful air. Then she noticed the sounds. Birdsong filled this new world, rich vibrant calls echoing from everywhere.

"Hey, easy, girl." The gunny tapped her shoulder. "You wanna limit that heavy breathing until your body adjusts. The air here has twenty-two percent more oxygen in it and gravity's only ninety-four percent of what you're used to. Doc said I should warn you. You're gonna find you're feeling much better, but you have to give it some time or you're gonna end up with a doozy of a headache."

They followed a well-groomed path over a peat-covered forest floor to the edge of the river valley. People were waiting on an overlook of the gorge. As they approached, a figure in light summer-dress uniform turned and began walking toward them, but Sara's eyes were on the skies behind the man. Bright, multicolored birds with long tails filled the heavens and valley below, swooping climbing and darting across the gorge as they called out impossibly complex melodies. Then she noticed that not all the flyers were birds. Most of them were brightly colored, but these strange creatures looked and flew differently. Their flight looked absolutely wrong. Their wings just didn't work right. Soft down, or maybe even fur, covered bodies with long necks, a round head, and long, pointy beaks. Their screeching calls sounded nothing like birdsong.

Alsoi's attention snapped toward Captain Tafton as he approached them. "Good morning, Lieutenant," he called out. "Nice to see you again.

"Good morning to all of you, I'm Captain Arlonious Tafton. I want to apologize for not greeting you sooner but I'm confident Gunny took care of your needs.

"First, come this way. You too, Lieutenant Alsoi, and please hold off on your questions. I need to show you a few things if you are to believe your circumstance."

The captain led them on a walkway that eventually took them out over the gorge. Solid railings provided safety, but even the Lieutenant needed a few steps to become accustomed to the transparent flooring. The shores of the river far below harbored herds of creatures. They traveled on two or four legs, seeming to live off the lush grass or leaves of the trees. A giant animal was swimming upriver. At first sight, Alsoi thought it was a huge reptile but then he noticed it had a long, smooth tail and flukes that drove it forward with amazing speed.

"There's going to be a lot to take in, so I'll let you lead the questioning," Captain Tafton offered. "Tell me. How do you like our home?"

"It's beautiful," Sara answered immediately. "Where exactly are we?"

"You are on Earth. I know that's not the answer you were expecting but … ah, I was hoping you would have a chance to see this. Look upriver, on the northern floodplain. See the herd? Several predators are tracking it. Focus on that clump of boulders at the base of the fallen Sequoia tree and watch for movement."

Jack's eyes suddenly opened, and the captain smiled. "Saw it didn't you? Ah I'm sorry but we haven't completed introductions."

"Jack Arlow, Ship's Engineer First Class, sir," Jack snapped to with a salute.

"You need not salute me, Mr. Arlow. We are not in the same service and our governments are not allies, but I thank you for the honor.

"Watch the boulders closely. There's a predator in there. They move very quickly and are masters of camouflage."

Sara let out a small squeak as something dashed out of the foliage. Running on two massive legs, a long tail trailing behind, it seemed to fly across the clearing. It launched an impossible leap that landed on an animal, that managed to sense the danger only at the last second. The victim was also on two legs but dropped to four just before the predator struck. A thick, skin-covered horn extended out from the top of its head, arching back over its brightly-feathered back. The victim let out a tremendous trumpet blast of sound that rang in their ears even at this great distance. Then the predator struck, ripping out its throat in a single savage motion. The entire river valley erupted in frantic calls echoing from the cliffs.

"Where the hell are we? This isn't Earth." Jerimiah's voice lifted above the bloodcurdling screams still rising from the distant riverbank.

"It's time for an explanation," began the captain.

"Welcome to Cretaceous Station. This is a research colony that is the home and birth planet of three nearby star colonies. They are …"

"No such thing exists," Sara Prakset interrupted.

"Oh? But they do," said the captain. "You can someday see for yourself. You are witness to our world, our technology and …"

Sara continued. "Earth has no colonies beyond those on Mars, Venus and the Belter's Biosphere. Even they can't get along."

"Yes, I know about the conflict," said the captain. "A sad situation but your eyes give proof. Here we exist and we are not a participant in those problems. Now please, no more interruptions. Let me explain.

"First of all, we cannot send you back to your Earth. It's not impossible. We occasionally return to our installation on Europa, but we cannot chance discovery.

"You each have a choice. You may leave Cretaceous Station at any time. Go anywhere in the world you wish. Of course, I wouldn't recommend it. As you saw in the valley, this is a savage world with horrors surpassing those just witnessed.

"You may also choose to leave and join a remote colony located a distance north of here. They have survived for more than a century and are doing quite well, but they are purists and prefer to live off the land rather than advance civilization.

"Finally, you can join us on our quest for the stars."

Jack Arlow spoke up, obviously upset. "You don't want to be discovered? Is that why you fired on us?"

"We didn't fire upon you," the captain replied. "We didn't even return fire when fired upon. I attempted a rescue of your ship but was only able to save your shuttle. That is why you are here, alive today. I believe Lieutenant Alsoi can confirm that."

"Aye," Alsoi replied. "It's as he says."

"Thank you," said the captain. "Let me explain how you arrived here.

"Our universe is several billion years old. There was a time when no matter existed, all was energy restricted to a single point. Even then the universe had creases in its ethereal fabric, physicists call them cosmic strings. Quite nasty things that you'd do well to avoid. You see, they're the width of about two protons. So much smaller than an atom in width but they extend for billions of miles and possess an immense gravitational pull.

"Now jump ahead a few billion years. As our solar system formed, it encountered a cosmic string tangled with a very tiny black hole that anchored it here in our system. Forces clashed. The string began spinning but was unable to break free of the black hole. Eventually, the opposing forces balanced into a high gravity, stable artifact.

"The high gravity artifact began sweeping up nearby matter, eventually forming into the so-called gas giant that we know as Jupiter. Jupiter is not a planet, it contains no solid material. It's a ball of vapors held captive by a microscopic black hole and sustained from collapsing to a single point by Hawking Radiation. The complex interactions of gravity between the cosmic string and black hole drive the immensely dense string in an unbelievably rapid spin."

"Bull," growled Jerry.

The captain chuckled. "Not sure I believe it all either, young man. Believe it or not, it gets better.

"Back in the late twentieth century, Doctor Frank Tippler theorized that an infinitely massive, long cylinder spinning along its longitudinal axis creates a frame-dragging effect that warps spacetime. The energy release tilts both space and time, forces the time component of a spacetime diagram to point backward or forward along the temporal axis.

"Any of that sound familiar? The spinning, immensely dense cosmic string we tracked inside the cyclone is a natural Tippler Cylinder.

"As we passed through the cyclone wall of the Red Spot, we entered a volume where the closer we approached and traveled along the cosmic string, the more rapidly back in time we progressed. Our exit brought us out here. Sixty-four or so million years earlier than the timeframe you were born into. Several hundred years prior to the extinction of more than eighty percent of all life on Earth.

"You now reside at the end of the Cretaceous epoch. Welcome to your new home, Cretaceous Station."

Sara had a flabbergasted expression on her face and looked like she still couldn't believe her ears. She blurted out, "You're kidnapping us?"

Alsoi still wasn't sold. "None of this makes sense. You said there's been a remote colony here for several hundred years. How did you get here then? We've had wavedrive capability for only twenty-five or thirty years."

"That's right," the captain replied. "It was the first interstellar ship that had the misfortune of discovering the true nature of the Red Spot and the good fortune to survive. They landed … Wait. Our director's coming."

All eyes turned to Hailey Sharpe as she approached. "Morning, Captain. Have you explained the situation to our new arrivals?"

"I was right in the middle of it, ma'am. I must say I didn't expect you'd be here."

"Oh tush. Do you really think I'd pass up the chance to meet people from my own time frame? I had a wonderful flight just listening to them discuss home."

Alsoi picked up on it right away. "You are from our time frame, but the station's been here for hundreds of years. Did you just …"

"No, Lieutenant. I was only fourteen when my family arrived."

"But, ma'am," Alsoi said, "that doesn't make sense either. Just how …"

Captain Tafton broke in. "Mister Alsoi, you should know better than to ask a lady how old she is."

"Oh, Captain," Hailey Sharpe said. "It's all right, Lieutenant. I'm two hundred thirty-seven years old and now that you've had the Nanobot inoculations, you can also look forward to a potentially long life. They do more than help you communicate and access our hive library. They also monitor and repair your body. We aren't sure of the ultimate lifespan yet.

"You will find that this is a very interesting place to live and grow old in. It's rather like that old Chinese curse, 'May you live in interesting times.' You see, there are many ways to die prematurely here. I can only guarantee you will not live a boring life."

"Why then don't you simply leave?," asked Alsoi. "You do have to contend with T-rex here and Lord knows how many other threats. Why stay?"

"Yes, I know you just saw a small T-rex. I'm sure there were several more, maybe dozens in the hunting pack down there. They are amazingly fast and cunning hunters."

"So, leave," said Alsoi. "Start your colonies on a distant star."

"We have started colonies but can't simply abandon Earth. At least, we can't just yet."

Screeching and hollering interrupted Hailey's speech followed by two muscular animals nearly as tall as the humans, and looking very much like brightly colored roadrunners. They arrived, charging over a bush-covered hill with the obvious intent of catching a much smaller bird that was barely knee-high, and even though brightly feathered, they obviously couldn't fly. Alsoi immediately recognized the larger animals as the two big birds they'd first encountered on the *Athos*.

One spotted the humans on the lookout and musically called to the other. Altering their course, they charged, only to brake at the edge of the cliff and cautiously walk forward. They walked with a very slow but graceful trot. When they reached Hailey, they began bobbing up and down, glancing alternately from Hailey to the new arrivals. Hailey smiled at her guests, absentmindedly running her fingers through the brightly colored ring of feathers on their necks.

The larger animal's head swiveled toward the humans, soft and quite flexible lips on its head moved to reveal a set of quite intimidating canines and molars set behind a small beak where a nose might have rested. It extended an arm and paw toward the lieutenant.

Hailey tapped it on the neck. "Francis, not now. They haven't met you yet.

She turned to Alsoi. "I'm so sorry, Lieutenant, but there's …"

Much to Alsoi's shock, words came out of the bird's mouth. "But you said we could speak with them after we came home."

The words floated in the air before the stunned humans. The sound seemed to emanate as much from the bird's throat as it did the mouth and lips.

Jack Arlow shouted, "They are talking birds?"

Hailey smirked. "Surely, Mr. Arlow, you're familiar with parrots. Many are capable of more than mimicry, you may wish to look up the research on African Grays of the late 20th century. They reported small parrots retaining vocabularies of several thousand words, quite capable of employing rudimentary logic.

"However, these are not birds, they are intelligent animals we call Hypsilophodon.

"Francis, now manners please when greeting Lieutenant Alsoi."

Francis walked over, again showed her teeth and extended an arm with a hand at the end of it that had four fingers and an opposable thumb. Alsoi simply stared at the hand. Francis looked puzzled and turned to Hailey.

"Lieutenant, Francis just offered to shake your hand," Hailey said. "Please don't be impolite."

"Well, my apologies, Francis," Alsoi said. "A handshake greeting is the last thing I expected." The contact was firmly gripped, although different from a human's hand.

"Thanks. Is alright, *Rootenant*," Francis cooed. "We must go, important work."

Hailey was chuckling quietly. "You've just met one of the natives. Francis is from a nearby colony of Hypsilophodon. They are not birds, but like birds, they are dinosaurs. They're one of the smarter species in this world. Although I find it increasingly hard these days to define intelligence.

"Like us, they are omnivores, they still exist here at the end of the late Cretaceous contrary to the paleontological records of your world. They have an opposable thumb and use crude tools much like the apes and birds of your world do. You would expect them to be quite civilized after more than seventy million years of evolution, but they are not.

"This species and so many others are intelligent but will never develop a creative civilization.

"Lieutenant, we all appreciate the help you gave so unselfishly. You were ready and nearly did sacrifice your life. Your actions were instrumental in turning back the latest alien attack but that wasn't the end of the threat.

"You see, we aren't the first humans to visit this early time. Way back in 2036 C.E., the first starship to leave Earth crashed into the Red Spot and disappeared. We know they survived the transit and landed on an Earth that was nearly a hundred million years younger than the land you now stand on. They went on to the stars, but a small contingent managed to return to Earth and their own time.

"In 2056 C.E. a leader of that original contingent returned here and landed at a nearby location creating our first outpost. I emigrated to that station as a child six years later and discovered a threat to our race that no one before me knew existed.

"Somewhere along the hundred or so million-year timeline between humanity's first landing and my arrival, our people must have managed to upset an alien species. Certainly nothing surprising for our species. Strangely enough, the aliens aren't even from our universe. So, why they care, how their species and ours first met, and what may have driven them to hate us so much remains a mystery.

"We do know they're from another cosmic brane or dimension and they have enough hate in them that they wish to eliminate humanity. I don't mean they want to kill off humans. After all, there aren't that many of us here in this timeframe or even in the home world you came from.

"From the vantage point of your century, Homo Sapiens as a species has been around for less than a million years. An extremely short timespan compared with the evolution span of most dinosaur species.

"Humans have had long-distance communications and telescopes for hundreds of years, and yet the universe appears empty. A great physicist of your time presented a theorem called Fermi's Paradox, that posed the conundrum that there are more stars in the universe than there are grains of sand in our oceans. With so many stars, where is everybody? We should see some evidence of other life. Yet there appears to be no life in this universe beyond our species.

"The citizens of Cretaceous Station have had interstellar capability for more than four hundred years. Considering all our colonies, exploratory missions, and deep-space interstellar drones, we have yet to find even a trace of another civilization in our universe.

"Oh, life abounds, even intelligent life like the Hypsilophodon, but not the creative intelligence that invents, constructs civilizations and dreams of flying between the stars. We think we know why.

"In a few centuries, this Earth will suffer the blow of a cataclysm known as the K-T or Cretaceous — Paleogene event that will result in the extinction of more than eighty percent of the species. Even more devastating for future life, this planet's climate will become unstable.

"Dinosaurs and the earlier life of this planet all enjoyed climate uniformity that changed very slowly. For billions of years, life evolved in a paradise-like, slowly changing environment with little challenge to their existence beyond their encounters with other species competing for the same food supply.

"The coming extinction will leave behind it a wild, harsh world. Temperatures and air composition will vary rapidly. Repeated ice ages will follow extreme cycles of hot climates that come and go in tens of millions, rather than hundreds of millions of years. Life here will be stressed repeatedly to the point of extinction by extreme climate cycles. The future you come from is a relative bio-desert compared to the Cretaceous Era with far fewer species and a miniscule animal population.

"In your home timeframe, more than ninety-nine percent of all species to emerge on this planet will have already gone extinct and the surviving species will pass into the ages after only a million or less years of evolution.

"Yours is a world cursed.

"Yet, the curse brings a blessing. Us. Humans.

"The stress of species competition combined with the challenges of a hostile environment ultimately resulted in the evolution of a race capable of meeting the challenges using more than physical adaptation. We did it by redefining the meaning of 'intelligence.'

"We alone have an intelligence capable of civilization and of dreaming of a future among the stars. Humans apparently are a rare and unique development in a very lonely universe. That brings us back to the aliens and their war on humanity.

"You see, we most likely are the only intelligent life in our universe just as the aliens are the only intelligent life in their universe. They see us as competitors and want to exterminate humans. Not just all humans, but all humans that have been and are yet to come.

"So, it is possible that the human species and its derivatives have existed among the stars for more than a hundred million years if our first expedition somehow managed to survive and evolve. We too are sending out colonies and if we survive then our ancestors will have inhabited and evolved on other stars for more than sixty-four million years by the time you are born. Our discovery of time-travel presents a unique problem for the aliens.

"Unfortunately, they have several potential solutions to the problem. They could completely sterilize our planet and ensure that life never evolves for the next sixty-four million years. If successful, then our species will never evolve and all humans, those past, present, and future, will cease to exist simply because they eliminated all life prior to the birth of our species. This solution encounters a big problem in that it's difficult to prevent life from evolving. Potentially a new species could arise presenting an even greater problem than Homo Sapiens.

"Alternatively..."

Alsoi broke in. "Nope. Doesn't work like that. Haven't you ever heard of the 'Butterfly Effect?' You change a simple incident and it influences all future history."

"Is that what you think, Lieutenant?" Hailey replied. "Have you been listening? Humans first landed on this planet a hundred million years ago. We are here now, and our future apparently remains the same.

"The researchers of Cretaceous Station had two hundred years to study this problem. Time isn't a table of billiard balls where altering the path of one item impacts all the others. Time is more like a stream or a river. Throw a stone into the river and a few ripples occur but they quickly fade and the flow remains. However, build a dam or block it with a tree and you can alter the course of the river.

"We believe they will attempt a similar remedy. Alter future evolution by preventing the dinosaur's extinction. Life here will continue in abundance with dinosauria as the dominant clade slowly evolving in a climate-stable world for eons to come. The dinosaurs will not only survive but continue, dominating and slowly evolving like they have for the past half-billion years. The climate stress needed to create our species will never arise. Humanity will never appear in the universe.

"The aliens would bring a much more peaceful future for the planet. These Hypsilophodon, we call them Hypes, are a sweet, gentle race. Only one of many that may continue to slowly evolve and survive for ages to come.

"I've personally traveled ahead to the moment of extinction. The Hypes will still exist and be flourishing as a species. On that day, their world will end abruptly. I witnessed it and heard the screams of the Hypes as they died, their voices rising to the heavens at the cataclysmic end of their species and so many others.

"If humans are to survive and evolve in the distant future of your birth, we must ensure the extinction happens. In saving our species, we will be directly responsible for the extinction of the dinosaur and so many other beautiful species.

"The concept haunts my nights. The memory of that visit rips my soul to this day and will continue until the day I die."

Hailey stopped and looked away from them to the peaceful sea. Her hand rose and rubbed something from her eye when a tiny, ladybug-like being emerged onto her shoulder. It began bobbing up and down, accompanied by the faint tinkle of bells. Hailey's quiet sob could barely be heard. "I'm okay, Tink. Now, go back. We'll discuss it later."

Hailey took a deep, sobbing breath and returned to her guests. "I'm sorry. Tink's my personal Bot. It's been with me a long time and has grown quite sensitive to my mood swings.

"Today, though, the sun is out. Dinosaurs sing and flowers have begun their emergence in a world of paradise. This is a fine day, a day of vast import for you. A day of decision.

"Will you join us on our quest to save humanity? A future where we guarantee the extinction of nearly all life on Earth, leaving behind a cruel world of climate stress, repeated extinctions and cruel death. If so, you will live with the knowledge that you are personally responsible for the loss of so many beautiful species and for ending a paradise.

"Our task continues after the extinction, for we must enforce the isolation and protection of our birth planet until that distant day when the cycle begins, and the first interstellar expedition of humanity sets out for the stars only to find itself sent a hundred million years into Earth's past.

"Or will you join the northern colony and live peaceful, exciting lives in this world knowing that you, your children and all your descendants will die in a hundred or so years along with the dinosaurs.

"The choice is yours."

"Why wouldn't you want to change the past? Why not?" demanded Nazir Khan angrily.

Herman Kahn Jr. stared passively. The questions stayed unanswered. He wasn't about to argue with his benefactor, the one providing the tens of millions his research demanded. All around them stood the evidence of that beneficence, the banks of computers, the nuclear accelerator, dozens of lab personnel, and the end result, the time viewer, tracker, and travel machine dreamt of since the days of HG Wells.

Nazir remained angry. He was not used to being even mildly challenged. At forty-five, he was young for a self-made billionaire. But work, stress, and worry left him looking old before his time, his eyes constantly red, his face heavily lined, his hair prematurely half grey, his body wiry and face gaunt from neglecting to eat. Herman was a decade and a half older but looked younger despite thick glasses and being heavyset and half bald. No worries for Herman other than the challenge of solving puzzles of abstract science and pure research. He naively never thought anyone would dare risk time travel and only wanted to view the past, not change it.

Herman said almost automatically, "There are dangers that have been in the literature since the earliest days of speculation. The Butterfly Effect and other conundrums that will, according to Bradbury and Asimov…"

"The mighty Asimov!" sneered Nazir. "Perhaps the only Jewish immigrant at that time who didn't lose family in the Holocaust. I wonder if he would have felt differently if he had."

"There are some dangers that would be catastrophic," continued Herman. "Time is a single stream existing only from past to present, not infinite streams including the future as some hoped for. And to travel to a time where you already exist would violate the principle that an object can't be in two places at the same time. It'd be as dangerous as bringing matter and antimatter together."

"That last one you need not worry about," Nazir replied. "Not for what I have in mind. And I will go forward with my plans, no matter the cost to me or anyone else."

Herman went silent, unwilling to alienate his boss. Nazir, as unhappy at not being challenged as at being challenged, continued his rant. It was obvious he'd thought much about the subject, and why he'd spent decades of time and much of his wealth making the research succeed. Nazir's following remarks sounded prepared.

"Why wouldn't you want to change the past?" Anyone with any humanity, with any sense of justice, would want to go back and change every wrongdoing, prevent every atrocity, every mass tragedy! Who would demand we do nothing? Lovers of the status quo like Bradbury the Midwesterner and Luddite! Privileged people born with a drawer full of silver spoons. People with not just a leg up, but a whole chorus line of Rockettes up on everyone else. People who fear disorder more than the worst horrors men have unleashed on each other. People who fear a just world because they might not be as close to the top anymore. Not even wealthy or powerful people, but those who want to be them, or trust them more than those who want change."

Nazir paused, probably realizing he was not winning the argument, but just being ignored. The lab assistants were going about their work. Nazir's security and yes-men were doing little but awaiting further orders. Herman tried gently broaching the topic, hoping to avoid debating principles so contrary to his own, which were purely abstract and thus not deeply held.

"Just what do you wish to do with the machine? When do you wish to travel back to?"

Nazir's eyes widened. He licked his lips before speaking and cleared his throat, so all would hear him. He clearly had been waiting a long time to say this to another.

"I'm going back in time to kill Nixon."

***

The room went quiet. Every worker stopped what they were doing. Most of them had been born after any memory of Nixon. But they were frozen in place, jaws dropped from hearing the open plotting of the assassination of a US president. Herman then saw that the puzzled looks on their faces meant everyone, like him, wondered about motive. Why bother killing a man already universally regarded as disgraced? It was like shooting a man jumping off a bridge.

Herman tried to lighten the mood. "You must really hate Republicans," he said with a forced laugh.

Nazir didn't laugh or even slightly smile. "I'm one myself," he said.

Herman didn't know what else to say. Slowly he began to say, "Then why…"

"I'm killing the man who caused the death of my father," said Nazir. "And I hope to bring my father back to life along with hundreds of thousands of others."

Herman's look was blank. So was everyone else's in the room. Nazir sighed and waved them all to come toward him. "You Americans. Time for a quick history lesson."

Nazir talked down to them like they were children. He had someone project a map with an outline over India, Pakistan, and Bangladesh, explaining the latter two were once one nation. He could have told them, "Google Bengali genocide." Instead he explained the actors in it, the death tolls, the atrocities in grim detail, and American ignorance and indifference.

Here was where Nixon came in. He helped the architect of genocide. Nixon admired Pakistan dictator General Yahya Khan as a strong anti-communist. When Yahya Khan started killing Bengali independence proponents by the hundreds of thousands, Nixon did nothing. When US ambassadors called for intervening, Nixon called them 'traitors' and removed them. When India's Prime Minister Indira Gandhi intervened, Nixon cursed her as 'The old bitch,' groused that Indians were inferior and bred too much, and sent weapons through Turkey, Jordan and Iran. He even sent the aircraft carrier USS *Enterprise* and a nuclear armed sub to threaten India.

Pakistan tried bombing India first, before Indian troops and planes could attack. "That bombing killed my father," said Nazir. "Attacks with American weapons killed the half of my family in Bangladesh."

"Would killing Nixon stop any of this?" asked Herman. "Why not Yahya Khan instead?" Herman wondered out loud, as if plotting a deceased president's death was illegal under US law. But surely not a Pakistani dictator.

"Always wanting to shift blame away from Americans," noted Nazir. "Yahya Khan sought Nixon's approval to bomb India. Without it, my father lives. Without American weapons, half the murdered Bengalis live. Killing Khan, especially by a Bengali, might convince other Pakistani generals to be more ruthless in slaughtering us."

"How would you even do this, get past Secret Service and White House guards?" asked Herman. He immediately wondered if he was implicating himself. But surely Nazir talking about this in front of dozens of witnesses was too reckless to actually be serious.

"You told me this is not just a time transporter, it is a transporter across great distances." Nazir smiled. "According to your theories, time travel has to be tied to the motions of the Earth, or you transport into cold space. So modifying this transport can put me any place on Earth, yes?"

Herman nodded. Nazir continued, "With great enough precision, I can land in the White House, any room I want."

"This speculation surely has gone far enough," said Herman in a low voice. "Don't you fear thirty people knowing what you plan?"

"No," said Nazir, his voice rising again. "For I know I will need all of their enthusiastic help to do this. And they know I can make them all wealthy! Who among you would turn down a flat fee of a million dollars each for a few weeks' work?"

The cheers of the assistants drowned out any objections Herman had. He started wondering which nations had no extradition, and could he learn the local language.

One of the assistants wondered if he could take Nazir's money, and still get more from the feds as an informant.

***

Three weeks later, Nazir was set to go. He was dressed as a White House servant, carrying a bottle of pure grain alcohol laced with poison to induce heart failure. Nazir also had an ice pick, a garrote, and a small size .32 caliber pistol, each in a different jacket pocket. Auto return was set to bring Nazir back from the same spot, twenty minutes after sending him.

The Lincoln Bedroom was empty that night, no international visitors in the historical record. Nazir slipped into the hallway and toward Nixon's study, where Nixon always drank alone.

Nazir started to enter quietly, then stayed behind the door. Nixon was falling asleep, already quite drunk, not noticing Nazir. "I'll get them…damn them all…" he said to himself. The man looked like he hadn't slept well in weeks. He was wearing shorts, but also a suit jacket and tie, and formal dress shoes with black socks held up by garters. Papers lay scattered about, some crumpled and torn. Nixon held up one page, blacking out sections. "Nixon can't say this," he said. The other hand pushed the play button on a cassette player. Nixon's own voice came out the speaker. He hit the record button to record over it.

Nazir stayed in the shadows by the opening of the door. The clock was ticking. He had less than fifteen minutes now. He wondered how long before Secret Service patrolled the hallway. Nixon kept rambling. "I never went to their damn Ivy League schools. I wasn't pretty like Kennedy. Didn't have the looks or money or time to fornicate. But they've had so much fun. A lot of fun kicking me around…"

Nazir hesitated. He had not expected to feel pity for this monster. He had the blood of millions on his hands, not just Bengalis, but Cambodians, Vietnamese, Chileans, Kurds, and 'my fellow Americans' all dying from his cold calculations. But Nixon was clearly tormenting himself as much as if he were in prison solitary.

Nazir steeled himself. The monster was only wallowing in self-pity, not caring about the nations he wrecked. This wasn't just about punishment and justice. It was simple practicality, kill one man to save many others, including family. *Think of your father you never met*, he thought. *Think of half your family, grandparents, aunts, uncles, cousins, all killed by Nixon's guns held by Yahya's thugs.*

His own gun would be too noisy. He hadn't intended to use it except as a last resort. Nazir wasn't sure if he had the stomach for the ice pick. He imagined the pick going into an eye or the gut, blood spurting everywhere, Nixon screaming and clutching himself, maybe in the ear or back of the head or temple. No, too much precision was required. There was only one way.

"Have another drink, Mr. President," Nazir said, lunging forward and forcing the bottle into his mouth. The poison was fast acting. Nixon started choking almost immediately, sputtering, "Damn breeders!" Nazir started strangling him with the garrote he brought, just enough to keep him quiet. The bony fingers of the most powerful man in the world clawed at him ineffectually. He finally went limp, then motionless.

Nazir stared into Nixon's cold, dead eyes. With a start, he realized he didn't feel any satisfaction or adrenaline rush from carrying out justice, just the fear of being caught. The study door was open. He heard another door creaking further back. Security!

He tiptoed to the study door and quickly, but gently, closed it. He listened quietly as the guard's dress shoes stepped on old carpet, paused by the study door, then kept walking. Trembling, Nazir brought out his pistol but dreaded the thought of shooting someone who'd never done a thing to him. The alternative was almost worse, a public trial followed by life in prison or the death penalty.

Nazir heard the sound of another door in the hall squeaking open.

He realized he had less than two minutes before the auto return point. The study door creaked as the guard opened it. "You!" yelled the guard.

Nazir started to run. He was unused to physical effort beyond pacing in his office. The quick run in sweaty servant's clothes was awkward. He felt a sharp pain, a joint in his leg pulling. He limped along quickly. The bedroom door closed behind him.

The auto return point was beginning to flash. He stood in it.

The bedroom door was opening. The guard ran in.

Nazir was back in the lab. Herman greeted him, surrounded by assistants. "How did it go?"

"No problems," lied Nazir. "Did it work? How is Nixon remembered in your memory, in this time?"

Herman said with puzzlement, "I still remember Watergate, the resignation, him trying to become respectable again with books and interviews…all of it."

Nazir was alarmed. "And I still have no memory of my father but photos. I still remember half my family murdered!"

The two men went to the time viewer. "This is very strange," said Herman. "There's more than a single time stream now. Two now, one of them breaking off from the original, right at the point you went back."

Herman searched for evening news of that night. Nixon's death was reported to be a heart attack, though conspiracy theorists were already raising questions. Herman found evening news of a year later. Some were tying it to the Kennedy assassinations, blaming Castro or the Soviets. VP Spiro Agnew fumbled around as president, was easily defeated in the '72 primaries by Reagan, who was then defeated by Edmond Muskie, who ended the Vietnam War quickly. Muskie kept the US out of the Bengali Genocide, except condemning it at the UN.

"I must find my father!" said Nazir impatiently. He pushed Herman aside and began scanning for the family home. He looked at Calcutta, 1971, at the Indian Army base. The viewer tracked down to a pilot's bungalow. Nazir breathed in deeply. He stopped.

Tears rolled down his face to see his father living…and carrying a baby boy! Nazir gazed at the image of himself held by his father. Whereas in his own timeline, his father had died before he was born.

"Leave!" bellowed Nazir. The room emptied. One assistant tapped the listening device he was wearing, trying to signal the feds.

Nazir viewed the life he and his father never had before. He saw himself growing up in Bangladesh instead of America and becoming a moderately successful economics professor. His father retired from the Indian military. Nazir married a woman he'd never met before. He saw his children and his father, the doting grandpa.

Herman timidly entered. Two security men had an assistant between them. Herman held a listening device in hand. "He's been informing for the FBI. What can we do now?"

"Pay the other assistants off," said Nazir. "But not to hide the crime. To say nothing of this invention. To protect themselves from prosecution. I will pay for their moves overseas. We must pack up the machine and viewer, and destroy everything else. You and I must run and hide to avoid a death sentence."

Nazir slowly paced. "I'm not done with this invention yet. Getting it built so I could save my family has been my goal my entire life, from the start of building my fortune. So I must do all I can with this time machine and stay one step ahead of the law. I can never visit this other time stream, can I?"

"No," said Herman. "The paradox would be disastrous. Letting you into a timeline where you already exist is as dangerous as letting matter and antimatter collide."

"I will always have this." Nazir pointed to the screen, at his more mediocre, but happier life. "The knowledge I saved my family across time, let my father live on in another reality. I'm his timely savior, and so are you. But I will never know him, be with him, speak to him. Like Moses viewing the promised land, fated to never live in what I've sought my whole life."

Dr. Elliot Cameron stood with dismay, facing the deserted beach that stretched from horizon to horizon in the glory of twilight. The superb beauty of the sight was not entirely lost on him. But proper appreciation of Nature's wonders is something heavily dependent upon circumstances—and these left a lot to be desired.

For the nth time he wondered what his real chances of being rescued were. They looked decidedly slim. But then he might be just taking the optimistic view. An hour earlier, he had felt happy to have escaped alive. Now he was beginning to have second thoughts.

It had been a close call indeed. Two minutes into the return leg of the trip the computer had flashed out the alarm, automatically bringing the ruined time machine back to normal time sequence, a mere couple centuries ahead. A siren had started to sound, piercing his ears.

Urged by his self-preservation instinct, Cameron had yanked the cabin door open and jumped out. He landed on his hands and knees. The sand rose in an ephemeral cloud all about him. He had then crawled frantically away. The complicated balance of forces driving the time machine fell apart in a blinding flash of light. When he dared to look back, the machine was gone.

Still in shock, he sat down awkwardly back on the warm sand.

Now what?

He was alive at least. Though the fact he was stranded on a still uninhabited stretch of the future Californian coast made him have more in common with the proverbial castaway than he cared to admit. He exhaled noisily in exasperation. *Or maybe not.* Even the much-overrated Robinson Crusoe had stood way better chances. After all, the guy hadn't gotten himself stuck three million years from home.

Sure, the travel had been a success—and a total disaster as well.

***

Cameron thought of the geologist's hoard he had so painstakingly stored away, enough to last him a lifetime of research. Unfortunately, it was stored aboard the now lost time machine. When he had set out to make the journey, he had wished only to return home with his precious cargo of rocks. He had been proud of himself then. Proud of a job well done. Full of confidence in the powers of technology. *Just a milk run, baby,* he had thought. *Now back home to a drink and a hot bath and bed.* It was the kind of pride that the gods frowned at.

And so, he embarked on the trip back—only to end up in a beach a mere two hundred years later, his time machine struck down by the forces it had dared to defy.

Oh my God oh my God oh my God...

The guys back at Caltech would eventually have to hit upon the obvious answer. He wasn't coming back at all. They would rightly assume the machine was destroyed or had somehow been rendered useless. In time, they might even be able to figure out what had gone wrong. Though right this moment, Cameron couldn't care any less if they ever did. He just hoped they would not assume him dead. He brushed the thought aside, with a shudder.

But of course, they'd try to find him first, wouldn't they?

They had that other machine at the Institute, the twin of his machine. And they certainly couldn't afford losing people in time missions. The very idea was adequately terrifying. History was already messy enough without outside help. There was no knowing what could happen if one wasn't careful. That was why, so far, all trips had been short. One-man ventures to nice, uninhabited patches in time to minimize risks.

So right now, a bunch of experts were probably thinking hard and fast. They'd throw together a rescue party in no time. That was for sure.

Yet come to think of it, they might just be in no particular hurry. After all, he'd always be here for them, no matter how long they took. Even in the (hopefully unlikely) event they decided to give the matter one or two generations of leisurely neglect until costs dropped. It wouldn't make any difference whatsoever.

Provided, of course, the accident had not already affected history in a way precluding any possible rescue.

The idea wasn't exactly thrilling. So Cameron decided he'd better assume a rescue party was on its way.

Only they would never know where to look for him— or was it when?

It was only natural, after all, that the search would be centered on the point of the past he had originally been bound for. They could not possibly be expected to know that the blessed machine had dumped him two centuries later than that.

Then again, the machine had just done its duty, and there definitely is a limit to what even the most careful programming can achieve. The all-important computer on board had learned of the impending danger of destruction of the vehicle and reacted accordingly in the only way its instructions had foreseen—by having the machine and passenger materialize at once in the three-dimensional universe again. That the point of departure had been left way behind was, all told, a minor incident in an otherwise perfectly well-handled emergency.

Too bad Cameron wasn't in the proper mood to appreciate the detail. When the rescue party got there for him, he wouldn't be around, of course.

Cameron groaned inwardly. He could easily picture a dumbfounded rescue party frantically trying to understand why he was nowhere in sight—or the machine, for that matter. Next, they would probably split into groups and start going over the entire sector of the coast with a fine-tooth comb. He did not feel interested enough to venture a guess at how long it would take for them to give up at that.

Easy there.

He might be overlooking something though. There was an angle he had forgotten about. Cameron frowned, trying to put some kind of order in the chaos of his ideas.

What if they did the smart thing? That is, look for him at any moment in time before he had started on his way back to the future?

So far, he had thought of that moment as a sort of a spot in a road, a place he had momentarily been in. But it wasn't so. Not at all. Time had indeed passed while he was out there collecting his damned rocks.

He had spent nearly twelve hours in the past. And any minute, any second at all of that period would do nicely. They only had to come and stop him from going back to the future.

It wouldn't matter if they got there ten minutes after his arrival, or ten minutes before his departure. They could even play it safe and come get him two weeks before his trip, or while he was still in college. It'd make no difference at all. As long as he was still there. So then he could be rescued—even before he was in any actual danger.

He had no sooner thought of it than he realized what a prize fool he was.

If that were true you wouldn't be here now in the first place, you moron.

He grew cold inside. If he was ever to be rescued at that time or any other moment in time, then the entire sequence of events leading up to his present plight would automatically cancel itself of course. He would never be here. He'd never have been here.

But then he was, naturally. That could only mean there had been—there would be—no rescue. Ever.

The sun was a red ball above the ocean now. Darkness would come in minutes. Cameron felt his pockets once more in the futile hope of finding something, anything, he hadn't found before. He stared dejectedly at the few possessions lying on the sand by him. A notepad. A ring of keys. A pen. A plastic canteen half-full of water. A comb. A candy bar.

He didn't even have a match on him.

The first mosquito droned for the attack.

***

Morning found him chilled to the bone. It had turned cooler sometime during the long night, his light shirt being no real defense. *October*, Cameron thought. *Hooray for sunny California.*

The night of sleeplessness had left him shattered. By some effort of will he'd managed to save half the candy bar for breakfast, along with some water. The rumblings of his stomach kept reminding him that it wasn't enough. Food, he decided somberly, was definitely going to be a problem.

Or not—he saw no point in merely staying alive. Not with three million years between himself and the world he would never again see.

And loneliness. Forever.

He had never been much of a joiner of anything, truth be told. But most of the time there had been somebody in his life, some girl or other. Not now, which was perhaps merciful. And there had always been friends—not many, not too close—and acquaintances, and colleagues. Someone to chat with, to keep him company over a drink. The feeling of people about him, if not actually minding him, but still. No one is wholly an island—that remains the privilege and the torment of God alone.

He sat up, facing the peaceful, indifferent sea.

Memories from his childhood days flooded his mind. A bottle washed ashore by a storm, and his disappointment that it contained no message from a desperate castaway.

He felt like crying. Now why should he suddenly remember this, out of his entire life?

He gnashed his teeth. At some more fortunate moment in history, he could himself have used a bottle to ask for help. In his present situation the idea was a stupid as could be. Nobody would be around for millions of years. And even then...

He almost stood up, stunned by the impact of the idea that had just occurred to him.

True, he had no way of sending a bottle across the ocean of Time to the future, even had there been any available.

But he could always try and send its equivalent instead.

The tides of Time could take to the coasts of the future any message able to withstand the beating of millennia. All it took was finding the proper way. In other words, he must find a way of marking this particular spot in time with an indelible sign—a sign that would perforce catch the eyes of researchers in the remote future. But how?

On an impulse, Cameron took out his pad, looked at it for a full second, nodded slowly to himself. A message, yes…

Suppose he buried a note detailing his plight deep enough so as to keep it from being unearthed too easily, too soon. His canteen would do nicely as a container. With a bit of luck, the message could survive until a time when people were able to understand its contents. Or, at the very least, pass it on to smarter generations as a riddle to be solved. They'd come for him, then, as soon as time researchers started looking for promising targets. Yes.

He wrinkled his nose.

No—that wouldn't do. That was deluding himself. The canteen he could more or less seal, of course, but then there was the inside air. It would start attacking the fragile paper the very moment he replaced the cap. In fact, air had already begun eating the paper the very second it was made. Over three million years, paper simply would become a nice layer of dust, as he could create no vacuum. End of the road.

He drummed his fingers on the pad still on his lap. All right, he could try burying something else instead— something anachronistic enough to get their attention. Such a finding was most likely to arise interest, debate, and eventually an investigation in detail. He quickly ran through his options in his mind.

Oh shoot.

Predictably, he had hit a wall again. The few items of clothing he had on were out of the question—nobody makes a shirt to last for millions of years. Metal rusted. Plastic would perhaps last a little while longer, though not a whole lot longer, it being biodegradable. That, by the way, disposed of the canteen scheme, another turn of the screw. He wondered dispassionately why he hadn't considered that before.

He grimaced. Hope had been slow to die, but now its agony was unbearably painful. None of man's proud creations stood a chance of weathering the merciless passing of Time. Whether he liked it or not, he was trapped, and death alone could affect the only rescue possible.

Cameron stood up, shaking all over as if with fever. He had a vision of his own bones bleaching under a fierce sun, beaten by winds and rains for centuries in a coast undisturbed but by the shrieks of seagulls—until their very dust became one with the sand.

And then, suddenly, it hit him.

Yes…

He had still, maybe, one way left, and again it came as a mild surprise to him why he hadn't thought of that sooner. The stakes were high indeed. Yet it was his only chance to call for help across the ages.

There is something no human being can avoid taking with him always—something that constitutes his mark as a member of a particular species, and that often outlasts the proud creations of humankind. Being denied the opportunity to leave other traces of his presence, he'd resort to his heritage yet to call for help. Throughout the ages, only the frail-looking product of blood and flesh had enough prestige to make itself heard.

To anthropologists in the remote future, the finding of fossil remains of modern man in the wrong geological strata would be a riddle, of course. Theories would succeed one another until the discovery of time travel allowed the question to be settled once and for all. Then, perhaps, Cameron could be rescued—rising indeed from among the dead.

All he needed to do was provide them with a nice skeleton. He had all the time in the world to arrange the details.

207

"Deux bières, s'il vous plait."

Le Lapin Soif was the third stop that evening during their Sunday pub crawl. Everywhere else was closed. Wood-paneling covered the walls, floors, ceiling, and even the bar, giving the room a dark atmosphere. A mottled statue covered in holes like Swiss cheese sat on the counter. One long ear extended from its summit, distinguishing it as what was once a rabbit. The booths were padded and comfortable. The tables spotlessly clean. Muttered sounds of conversation could be heard everywhere, masking Nicki Minaj singing "Bang Bang" over distant speakers and the rain tapping on the roof.

Giles stood, looking imposing in his black security uniform. Yet he was overshadowed by his statuesque best friend and drinking companion, André, who'd just requested a couple cold ones.

André waited for their drinks at the bar while Giles found an empty booth. When André returned with their Molsons, his eyes were wide with excitement. "Are you serious, mec? A working time machine?"

Giles chugged his beer quickly. "Can't we talk about something besides work?" His head was already starting to ache. "I spend enough time in that lab babysitting the professor and her shenanigans."

No sooner did Giles drain his Molson then André fetched him another. Giles noted André was still sipping his first. André leaned back into his seat, his flannel shirt billowing loose from his blue jeans. His lips curled into a devious grin. He looked for all the world as if he'd just won the lottery. "You can't just bring up time travel and drop off."

Giles consumed his nepenthean beverage. "Seriously, it's nothing. Just a huge, silver golf ball."

While André signaled a waitress, he asked Giles, "Does it really function? I heard it was a scam."

"It's the real deal." Giles downed the rest of his glass.

"But what about that press conference? I saw it on television. Didn't they just mock up two balls to give the illusion of travel? That's what the reporters said."

Giles lowered his voice. "Seen it with my own eyes. The professor took me on a trip once. Took me to see the Gettysburg address since she knows I'm a big Lincoln fan." Giles shrugged. "But what's it matter? I like the here and now. I like antibiotics. The past is the past. We live in the present, and that is the best time to be."

André nodded slowly. "Well, yes, but…" He leaned in close. "Haven't you even been tempted to take it for a spin? I mean, it's a *putain* of a Time Machine! Think of what you could do with that? You could kill Hitler, or Stalin, or Mao!" André took another sip. "Or all three!"

"The professor says we can't change time. It's too dangerous." Giles finished his fifth beer. He was surprised to see that his companion was still on his first as the waitress brought another. "Why aren't you thinking… I mean drinking?"

André waived his hand. "Mec, this is serious." He took another sip. "Can I see it?"

Giles tried to shake his head, but wasn't sure if he was being clear. "The professor tends to sleep in that laboratory. It's why they have us guarding it." He slammed his beer and André commanded another.

André took his time as he imbibed. "Was she there when you finished your shift?"

Giles put down his glass and struggled through his drunken haze to focus. *Brain, you know this!* But finally, he had to admit, "I don't remember."

"Time to settle up, gentlemen," the server interjected. "That'll be thirty dollars." She took the bills Giles proffered and handed him back a ten.

Giles's hand trembled as he held the change, contemplating the banknote. He turned it over and over, pensive, settling on its obverse. There was something about that face. "John A. MacDonald, the first Prime Minister."

André winced. "He's no Prime Minister of mine!"

"Sure, he's no Lincoln, but he united us as Canada."

"This is Québec!" André pointed to the provincial flag hanging behind the bar. "All they ever do in Ottawa is shove English ways down our throats. It's bad enough this city is overrun by Anglophones."

"We're nowhere near Notre-Dame-de-Grâce, and even there, the signs are still French. The by-election's over. You lost the riding." Giles wiped the beer drool from his lips. "Cut out the electoral rhetoric. I'm no constituent you need to convince. Just be glad it's all over and you don't have to shake any more grubby hands and kiss any more colicky babies." Giles pointed to MacDonald's ear. "This election changes nothing. Québec is French and will be long after we're dead, whether Québec remains a part of Canada or not."

André yanked the ten-dollar note from Giles's hand and struggled unsuccessfully to rip it up. "*Merde!*" Frustrated, he soon gave up and used a pocketknife to cut it in two. Sweat beaded from his dark, receding, unruly hair and bulbous nose.

"Careful!" Giles took the pieces of money, smashing them together. "This security job barely pays enough for libations." He shoved it in his pocket. "Next time, you pay. You're the lawyer."

André took a final swig, finishing his first beer. "Let's go."

"Where?" Giles stumbled from his seat.

"You'll see."

Giles was too drunk to protest as André led him under the Rue Saint Denis streetlights, a cold drizzle accompanying them. They'd cinched their collars tight, avoiding puddles.

André stopped in front of the university physics building. "We're here."

Giles had already moved on ten paces before he noticed his friend had stopped. As he turned, he started to lose his balance, so he grabbed the wall. "But this is where I work."

André went to his friend and seized him by the shoulder. "You're in no state to make it home. Best we go in here so you can rest." André cinched Giles up as he began to sag. "Plus, you can show me the ship."

Giles sighed. "You got me drunk just to see the ship?" He sniffled.

"Steady on. I'm just trying to keep you from catching a cold, my friend."

Giles fished the key from his belt. As the door opened, Giles started to fall through.

André grabbed him. "Okay, mec, which way now?"

"Room 317." Giles rested his eyes.

At the stairs, another guard was pacing the halls. "Giles, is that you?"

Giles squinted. "Oh, François, yeah. This is André." Giles pointed in the general direction of his friend.

André held out his hand. "Pleased to meet you."

François stiffened. "Oh, hello, sir. I voted for you."

Giles began to slouch.

André grabbed his friend.

"You okay, mec?" François put a hand on Giles's shoulder.

"It's fine. I just need to check on something. We won't be here long." Giles tried to stand but had to use the wall for support.

François nodded and headed off in the opposite direction.

His companion dragged Giles upstairs and to a nondescript door on the third floor. André peeked in the darkened window. "I don't see your professor."

Giles fumbled to unlock the room, stumbled in and groped for the light switch. The professor's laboratory was an expansive, white experiment hall with picture windows and tables for students interspersed throughout. In the back, near the door, there was an empty couch. The sphere lay at the head of the chamber.

André whistled. "*Chouette*. It's like a miniature Epcot!"

"Okay, now you've seen it. Let's get going." Giles grabbed the back of the closest chair to steady himself.

"Wait," André said. The ball was practically twice André's height. He struggled with a door etched on one side. "Locked."

"Get away from that." Giles's eyes widened, though he had trouble focusing. Panic screamed through his thoughts. *He's gonna get me sacked!* Giles pushed up, and started to move forward but lost his balance, grabbing another desk to keep from tumbling.

"So, where do you think she keeps the key?" André spotted a glint of metal on the front desk. "Aha!"

"Stop." Giles shifted up and wobbled closer. He halved the distance before the world spun again.

André took the key and turned it in the device's lock. The door swung open revealing a velvet red interior with seating for six around a central console. He stepped inside then beckoned. "Coming?"

"Get out of there!" Giles steadied himself, finally reaching his companion. He tried to extract his friend, but André had better purchase and yanked him inside. Giles collapsed on the floor, shutting his eyes, listening to André speak above him.

"How do you turn this thing on?"

Stop…

"Oh, cool! That looks like the right year…"

Giles willed his arm to move without success.

"Romeo and Juliette! Perfect."

His world went blank. Giles's dreams were troubled.

***

Why am I shaking? Giles wondered.

"Mec, wake up!"

Giles was lying on the red, velvet cushions of the ship, his head aching, though most of his drunken fog had cleared. "What happened?"

"Shall we have a look outside?" André opened the door and Giles tumbled onto a muddy, sylvan outcrop, stopped by a sugar maple tree. A midday sprinkle pattered gently.

Giles rubbed his eyes. "Where the heck are we?"

"Montréal, Québec. Can't you tell?" André exited the ship and locked the door. He put the key in the pocket of his jeans.

Giles took out his iPhone 5S. There was no signal and not even the satellite maps could load, never mind give his location. "This can't be Montréal. Even Parc Royal doesn't have this many trees."

"It did once." André grinned, winking.

Giles shook his phone, then put it back in his pocket. "You haven't?" Giles gaped. *How am I going to explain this to the boss?*

"Welcome to 1864, *mon ami*."

Giles tried to pry open the door. "Mec, you've marooned us here. How are we going to get back?"

André shrugged. "I noticed a quick return button when I was getting us here. We can try it when we want to get back, but first, let's explore." He grabbed Giles's arm and pulled him from the ship.

"But why did you have to bring me?" Giles shivered.

"You said yourself you'd been to the 1860s before. I needed a guide."

"I don't know anything about the 1860s!" Giles trembled, rubbing his arms. "You couldn't at least pick a warmer month for this insane bit of tourism?"

"What do you expect for early October? Isn't it wonderful. So much to see. So much to say…"

Giles's teeth started chattering. He was caked in dirt. His head ached. "I need a drink."

"Well then, let's get some," André replied. "You think Le Lapin Soif is still around?" André directed them toward Place Jacques-Cartier. As they exited the park, the streets were bustling with pedestrians under parasols and horse-drawn carriages. The air was thick with woodsmoke.

"What's that smell?" Giles held his nose as they passed the Hôtel de Ville and headed toward Rue Saint Denis.

André snorted. "And I thought car exhaust was bad. Watch your step."

Le Lapin Soif was barely more than a lean-to sitting among its roughshod, wooden neighbors. A Union Jack hung behind the bar, and an intricately carved and lacquered wood statue of a rabbit sat on the counter, shining as if new. People stood, milling about in the open air, with nondescript green bottles in hand.

André waved down a pretty, young barmaid. "Deux bières, s'il vous plait," he requested.

"That'll be twenty-five cents," the barmaid replied.

Giles whispered, "We don't have 1860s currency."

André shrugged. "Just give her a toonie."

The barmaid examined the coin carefully. "Peculiar coinage and peculiar fashion sense. Not from around here, eh?" She took a heavy tome from under the bar and flipped through it, looking for a match. "This piece be not issued from any bank I recognize. What is it, some golden eye of brass with a white bear?"

"It's a toonie," Giles offered nervously. "It's worth $2."

"I doubt that, but I guess the metal must be fair trade." The barmaid handed them two beers.

Giles pursed his lips as he sipped the vintage beverage. "They call this Molson? If all 1864 has to offer is warm, questionable beer and horse manure, I'd just as soon we finish our drinks and go. This place is giving me a nightmare chill."

André protested. "But there's a play I want to see. Maybe some constitutional delegates will be there!"

"Delegates? You idiot, this is Montréal. In October 1864, the Québec Conference was in Québec. Ville Québec."

André winked. "Ah, but on this day there's supposed to be a major performance. Shakespeare's Romeo and Juliet."

"*Putain!* You could see that back in 2014!"

"But in 2014, you don't have John A. MacDonald."

Giles shook his head. "If you wanted to see him, why didn't you just take us to the conference in Québec? For that matter, why not just take us to Charlottetown?"

André grunted. "The ship's hard to pilot."

"What?"

André ignored the question, turning to the barmaid. "Which way to the Theatre Royale?"

She pointed toward the river. "Oh, just down the road, by the port of Montréal. You can't miss it. And you're right, I did hear Mr. MacDonald is in town for it. Came in on a steamer this morning, down from Ville Québec."

"See." André nudged Giles. "Come on!" He led his friend down to the shore. The Vieille Porte was anything but old. New construction was everywhere and marble and granite gleamed as the sun finally made an appearance from behind the clouds.

As they approached an ornate building, a man with a thick beard spotted André and tried to intercept. "Hey, Johnny, what're you doing here? Didn't I just see you inside? And what the heck are you wearing?" He stopped a few paces from André. "Oh, excuse me sir, you look just like Minister MacDonald."

"That's quite all right," André smiled as he replied in English. "The name's Andrew Smith, Lieutenant of the United States Army, on leave from the Maine First Infantry, and this is my traveling companion, Mark." He indicated Giles, who joined them sheepishly.

The man with the thick beard beamed at them. "Pleased to meet you, Lieutenant. Oliver Mowat at your service. I swear, though, the resemblance is uncanny."

André brightened. "That's great. I loved Born Naked."

Giles punched his companion lightly. "You're off by about a century, mec. That's Farley Mowat. This is one of the constitutional delegates!"

André nudged Giles. "Bien jouer!"

"Good sirs, if you'd not consider it too much a burden, would you kindly accompany me inside? I'm sure Mr. Brown will find your aspect rather amusing."

Giles and André followed a few paces behind Mowat into the theatre.

"Hey," Giles whispered to André, "why did you tell him you were a soldier?"

"I always wanted to play a soldier." André whispered back, a wide smile on his face.

"You and your community theatre." Giles rolled his eyes. "Don't you think we should keep inconspicuous?"

André shrugged and rushed to keep up with Mowat.

Outside the theatre, Giles spotted the playbill. 'Romeo et Juliet, avec M. John Wilkes Booth de Bel Air, Maryland, É.U.' Upon the parchment was a drawing of the actor in period garb.

A woman strode up next to Giles. "Isn't he spectacular? So handsome."

Giles scoffed and strode through the wide theatre doors. He found André inside the open gallery, ahead of the main entrance. Mowat was talking to Minister MacDonald, along with two other historic statesmen Giles recognized, George Brown and George-Étienne Cartier.

Mowat quickly introduced André and Giles to the group. "I fear my seats will not be as good as yours, good gentlemen," Mowat said. "I will find you after the performance." He bowed as he left.

Cartier spoke to them in near-perfect English. "Oliver's quite right, it really is most extraordinary."

MacDonald gestured for the group to follow him. "Come on, lads, let me get you some drinks." MacDonald led the party of five back to a dry bar to the side of the lobby.

Brown resumed his conversation as they walked, addressing Cartier. "Do you think you can convince the Canada East contingent to support the principles we've laid out?"

"No, don't agree!" André interjected. "What they're proposing is a shackle around the neck of the French-speaking majority."

Cartier lifted an eyebrow. "Harsh words from an American. What do you know about French culture?"

André replied, "The French are special. They're a unique culture that you guys just want to subsume by some chiefly English central government."

Giles grabbed a drink, then shook his friend's arm. "What're you doing?"

"Fixing history," André whispered.

"With all due respect, Lieutenant," MacDonald began, "as a guest in our nation for whatever purpose, it's because of your nation's past interference in our sovereignty that we need a strong central government to stand up to unbridled American expansionism." MacDonald finished his beer and poured another, then turned to leave, followed by Cartier and Brown.

"Wait!" André chased after them but was stopped at the Theatre doors.

"Tickets?" A man dressed in livery stopped André at the gate.

"How much for one ticket?" André asked.

"Five dollars, and you can get one at the front of the theatre, if there's any left."

André turned to Giles. "You got any more toonies?"

"Not that many!" Giles's head began to throb. He knew he hadn't had enough water to hydrate. *Damn hangover!*

"Merde!" André stormed out the door.

When Giles caught up with his friend, he was at the side of the building. Above the door where André was trying to get in, there was a sign marked 'd'Entre Étage.'

"Mec, what are you doing?" Giles asked.

A stagehand strode up behind them.

André turned to the stagehand. "I forgot my key."

The stagehand glanced them up and down, then shrugged. He opened the door and let them pass. "Serendipitous haberdashery. Can't wait to see the play."

Inside, Giles followed André into the dressing rooms. The halls were dark, lit only by candlelight. They had trouble seeing their way.

"How dare he walk off before I was finished." André fumed. "The temerity of him!"

"Well, MacDonald was our first Prime Minister," Giles replied.

"We'll see about that!" André passed a door with a dimly illuminated plaque where a large, yellow star was inscribed. Behind the closed door, they could hear folks talking.

"Times are desperate. If we take St. Albans, we can break Grant's back by forcing him to split his forces and lay off the heart of the Confederacy. And we can loot the banks to help fund the war effort. Plus, with your notoriety, we're sure to win the hearts and minds. The South shall be free of the Yankee yolk of oppression!"

Giles hesitated. That had to be him. Opportunity was knocking. *Dare I? Kill John Wilkes Booth before he can assassinate Abraham Lincoln?*

"What are you doing?" André grabbed Giles's arm and propelled him forward. "We need to find the costume chamber."

Giles stared back at the door as his friend dragged him forward. "But it's John Wilkes Booth. He's right there?"

"So what? Do you think you can just walk in there and save Lincoln's life?" André stopped in front of a doorway lit by candlelight.

"Well, yes. I mean, I suppose." Giles shrugged. "But I guess you're right." Giles didn't have the heart to kill anyone.

Inside the room, there were rows and rows of clothes hanging from wooden dowels. André was zigzagging through the room, riffling through various fabrics. He stopped at a contemporary—for 1864—costume. It was a facsimile of what they'd seen John A. MacDonald wearing earlier. "Perfect!" André cried.

"What are you doing?" Giles said in a harsh whisper.

André began to disrobe, then put on the Victorian suit. "How do I look?"

Giles pinched his temple. "You look just like him."

"Exactly. If MacDonald won't listen to me, maybe I can convince Cartier."

"You mean you intend to impersonate him?" Giles shook his head. "I don't think that's wise. Anyway, won't MacDonald try to stop you?"

André smirked. "Not if I can drink him under the table."

"That doesn't work!"

"It did on you." André shrugged and headed out the door. "Come on, let's find MacDonald's balcony."

Giles's head began to ache again as they wondered up a corridor, looking for a way to the audience seating.

Finally, they came upon the stage. The set was still being configured and the curtain was still down.

André approached the drapes. "Come on."

Giles followed André onto the boards. On the floor, a few of the stage candles had already been lit, but most of them were dark. The gallery was in shadow and Giles couldn't see where MacDonald was seated. Beyond the platform, the orchestra pit sank about one and a half meters.

André was bowing and spinning for the audience. The crowd began to laugh.

"You there! Stop mocking me and get up here!" cried a voice. It was MacDonald, and it'd come from the first balcony on the left.

André rushed to the end of the stage, came down the stairs and then into the aisles, followed closely by Giles.

Eventually, they found Brown, Cartier, and MacDonald seated in their private enclave. One chair was empty.

MacDonald rose. "Ah, there's my doppelgänger. Come over here sir! Mr. McGee wasn't able to make it. Please take his seat."

Mr. Brown rose as André sat, then pointed to Giles. "Here, good sir, have my seat. I shall see if Mr. Mowat still has a place adjacent." He nodded to his companion. "Be well, gentlemen. I shall seek you upon final curtain."

Giles took the seat next to Cartier as Brown exited.

On stage, a boy began lighting the rest of the stage candles. The audience went silent. The curtain opened to a set draped in a renaissance interior room with two actors. The actors waited for the applause to subside, then began their dialogue.

"Gregory, on my word, we'll not carry coals."

MacDonald drew a flask from his inner pocket. "Care to share a drink, good sir?" He handed the beverage to André.

André shot Giles a mischievous look, then took a quick swig. His eyes went wide. "That's the good stuff!"

MacDonald smiled. "Glad to see you share my taste as well as my aspect. Perhaps we were too hasteful in our recriminations." MacDonald grabbed the container and took a drink himself.

André nudged MacDonald. "It's nothing a little alcohol can't cure, eh?"

MacDonald cleared his throat. "Now, good sir, would you mind I beg to inquire, for what reason do I detect a moderately french drawl in your speech? Did you not say you were of Union blood?"

André grinned and took another swig. "Ah, good question. As I said, I am from Maine, northern Maine, and we do speak the old language there, *n'est pas?*"

MacDonald and Cartier both chuckled.

Cartier leaned in and whispered. "I see why you stand so affirmatively with the French of Lower Canada, mon ami." He drew back and crossed his arms. "But be rest assured, we wish to form a pluralist society where French and English are equal in rights and privileges."

MacDonald gulped down a mouthful of booze. "Enough politics, good sirs. Are we not here on a night free of debate? Save the discussions of sovereignty for Québec. May we enjoy our liberty…" He handed the bottle back to André. "…and libations!"

Thank goodness, Giles thought to himself. *Enough with the politics, André!*

As the story played out on stage, André and MacDonald continued to pass the flask between them.

Not far into the third scene of Act One, the bottle was dry. André turned to Giles. "Mec, get me another drink from the lobby."

Giles glared at his friend. "We still don't have any money!"

MacDonald chuckled. "Oh, lad, just tell the barman I sent you and to add it to my tab."

When Giles got to the dry bar, sure enough, upon mentioning MacDonald's name, he was able to get a new bottle which the bartender opened for him. When he returned to the balcony, André and MacDonald were laughing, though Cartier sat sternly, seemingly engrossed in the play.

Each time they finished, Giles was sent to fetch another beer. By Act Five, Scene Two, MacDonald and André were both nearly falling out of their chairs.

"*Anoffer*," MacDonald slurred drunkenly .

As Giles was getting the drink, he saw Cartier rush out of the theatre. When he returned to the balcony, one of the MacDonalds was pummeling the other on the floor. Giles couldn't tell which was the real MacDonald and which was André. Giles tried to pull the aggressor off the victim. He assumed the attacker was André. He knew his friend's temper.

André continued punching, ignoring Giles.

Just then Cartier returned with a constable.

The constable raised his handgun. "Get off of Mr. MacDonald, you American spy!"

Giles backed away, keeping clear of the weapon.

"This is your last warning, sir!" the constable said in firm tones.

André ignored him, continuing to beat MacDonald.

The officer fired. André collapsed. Dead.

The theatre went silent as everyone stared back at them.

Cartier rushed forward and scooped up MacDonald, spiriting him away.

The constable blocked Giles's escape.

An actor cleared his throat, continuing with his lines. "Give me that mattock and wrenching iron."

Giles backed away. He could feel the balcony behind him.

"Hold, take this letter. Early in the morning see thou deliver it to my lord and father."

Giles jumped from the balcony. He landed on stage, face to face with Romeo. Face to face with John Wilkes Booth.

"Give me the light." Booth turned to an actor holding a torch, ignoring Giles.

Giles's fist was in the air before he realized what he was doing. It connected squarely with Booth's jaw. "That's for killing Lincoln!"

Booth started to tumble but then did a backflip. However, when he landed, his foot knocked over one of the stage candles and he tripped, falling into the orchestra pit, the torch flying from his hand. Bloody fingers emanated from his head, staining the concrete.

Fils de chienne!

The stage candle, which Booth had kicked, had begun to light the stage on fire. At the same time, the curtain started burning, having caught flame from the thrown torch. There was pandemonium as the audience tried to rush from the theatre and the other actor ran to the wings.

Giles ran backstage and tried to find his way to the stage door. It felt like the fire was licking his boots as he made his way through the darkness. Eventually, he found the door and exited to the street. It was nighttime.

This can't be happening!

In the alley, he was swamped by people trying to escape the scene. He had nowhere to go. He wandered aimlessly, anonymously, trying to avoid anyone in uniform. The black of his clothes helped him blend into the dark.

Finally, exhausted, Giles stumbled upon the machine they'd arrived in, still nestled among the trees. The door was locked. André had the key. Giles paced in front of the vessel. *I'm trapped in the past! Trapped and alone!*

He'd have to go back. He'd have to find André's body and look for the key. Giles shivered at the thought of returning to the conflagration. He sat against the sphere. Giles could see the lights from the inferno through the trees. He didn't know how much of the Vielle Porte he'd destroyed, or how he could even search the wreckage for a small key.

He yawned. At least they were parked someplace quiet. Giles shut his eyes.

***

Giles awoke next to the sphere, covered in mud and moss stains. He stretched and shook his head. He was cold and hungry. He was lying next to a huge, silver golf ball.

He remembered.

Giles sighed and stood, then made his way back to what remained of the theatre. *If I don't find the key, maybe I can get a job? Maybe a merchant marine? A dock worker?*

Giles gasped as he approached the destruction. The entire district where the theatre had stood was now haphazardly strewn with stone and ash.

Urchins scurried among the debris.

Giles traced his path to where he thought the balcony had stood, and moved the soil with his foot, looking for a glint of metal.

Some of the young scavengers started to move toward him.

He gave them what he hoped was a brutal stare.

They backed off.

Giles fell to his knees as he tried to get a better look at the ground. If he could only find some unburnt fabric, a bone, a gold tooth. He sighed. They probably already picked the area clean.

He just sat there, staring across the St. Lawrence river. Forsaken.

He felt a hand on his shoulder.

"I'd hoped I'd find you here, Mec!"

Was he hallucinating? It sounded like… "André?" Giles stood and faced his friend. "But, but, you were dead. I was there. That *flic* shot you?"

André laughed. "Actually, he shot MacDonald. You just assumed I was the one doing the beating. Seems MacDonald could hold his beer better than me."

"And Cartier?"

"I just let him go on thinking I was MacDonald. I tried to convince him to forget this Confederation idea, but he just assumed I was concussed or something." André rubbed his scalp, pushing back his unruly hair. "Said he was going to inform the Queen of the assault."

"Where is he now?"

"Probably half way up the St. Lawrence, back to Ville Québec with the rest of the delegates." André shrugged. "I gave some excuse about seeking local medical care and told them I'd join them later."

Giles hugged his friend. "I can't believe it! I thought I was trapped here forever!"

"I'm surprised you didn't leave without me. I didn't see you at the sphere. I've been looking for you all morning."

Giles stepped back, glaring. "I don't have the key."

André padded his pockets. "Oh, right." He fished out the key. "Let's go!"

They climbed the hill back to the ship and got inside. André found a red button marked 'quick return.' The ship made a horrible wind before rumbling into motion. As the sounds of 1864 faded, the chirps of long dead morning birds echoed like ghosts through the ages.

***

The dust settled in the university laboratory as the ship fell like expanding spaghetti from a three-dimensional projection of some 150 years earlier. By the time the image disappeared, the machine had expanded to its full size and André shoved the door opened.

Giles rushed out. "I need a drink. Coming?"

André exited, locked the door, then replaced the key. "Absolutely! It's a new day!" André slapped Giles on the back and they headed into the hall.

Locking the door to room 317, Giles noticed it was dark outside. He sighed. "That was 1864. Here it's definitely still night."

André grinned. "Just like when we left. At least it's stopped raining."

"Hey, Giles, is that you?" a voice called from behind them. "You feeling better?" They turned around. It was François.

Giles chuckled. "Never felt more alive in my life, François! Never felt better!" Giles could feel André's smile. It was contagious.

François approached them. "What happened to your uniform? How did you get it all muddy after only ten minutes in here?"

"Freak mud storm?" Giles said. "I'll see you tomorrow, François."

They made their way out the building, onto the street.

André pointed down the street with his chin. "Why don't we see if Le Lapin Soif is still open. My treat this time!"

"I was so worried I'd lost you!" Giles was positively giddy.

They made their way up Saint Denis but stopped short at the sign reading 'The Thirsty Rabbit.' Giles hesitated.

André strode through the tavern doors confidently. "Coming?!"

Eventually, Giles followed André in, finding him at the bar.

"Deux bières, s'il vous plait." André ordered.

"What? Sorry, sir, I couldn't understand you." The bartender spoke English.

"This is Québec. We speak French here." André replied in English.

"French? They haven't spoken that in Quebec State since, what, the 1860s?" The bartender chuckled. She'd pronounced the state with an English *kw* sound.

André blanched.

"The 1860s, you say?" Giles inquired. "What happened then? Besides the American Civil War."

"Don't you guys know your history? Some anarchist assaulted some Canadian politician during the war, driving him mad, and they blamed the Union. Queen Victoria declared war on us."

"You mean the U.S.?" Giles cut his eyes toward André as an image of the other MacDonald lying dead on the balcony flashed before him.

"Yeah, but the South was already on the ropes, so once Lee signed Appomattox, Lincoln directed the Union armies north. He took Canada, which was still bickering over its autonomy with England, and restored order."

Giles descried a flag. It bore thirteen red and white stripes and a blue field of stars, nine by five with four stars on the top and bottom. "Fifty-Three stars…"

"Of course," Giles said. "Ontario became a state first, in 1881 and Quebec became the fortieth in 1885."

Giles contemplated Booth, in the orchestra pit, bleeding to death, flames all around. He recoiled and his stomach sank. "What about Lincoln?" he asked. "Wasn't he assassinated in 1865? Someone must have sought to kill him besides Booth."

"Lincoln?" The bartender furrowed her brow. "No, he died in, I think, 1886 in Illinois. There weren't any chairs or booths involved. I think he died peacefully in his sleep."

André pulled Giles aside. "This is bad. Mec, this is incredibly bad." André shuddered.

"John A. MacDonald's dead. It's all your fault." Giles folded his arms.

"So let's go back. We can stop ourselves. Prevent MacDonald from being shot." André's eyes shifted from side to side.

"We can't do that. It would create a paradox. If we influence our past actions, the consequences could be catastrophic." Giles grabbed André, trembling. "There is no shake to undo. We have to solve this without changing our own past."

André slipped free of Giles's grasp. "There must be another way."

Giles shut his eyes and slowly shook his head. He took the lavender fragment from his pocket. The ten-dollar bill still bore MacDonald's portrait, just as before. He handed it to André. "You know what you have to do."

André shook his head. "You expect me to go to the Québec Conference and take his place? I refuse!"

"They don't even speak French in Québec anymore!" Giles insisted. "You have to!"

André fell back, fear burning in his eyes. "I can't. I can't take his place."

Giles smoothed André's hair like MacDonald's. "I don't think you have a choice."

"But you're asking me to be the biggest traitor to Québec sovereignty in history."

"*Ta gueule!* I…" Giles stammered. "I have to kill Abraham Lincoln."

"Where the hell are we?" Mayor whispered a bit too loud.

"It's a cemetery, inside a mausoleum and keep your voice down." Gina gave him an elbow in the darkness. *At least he had followed protocol and kept his left hand on her shoulder as they transitioned through the portal.*

A small device lit up in her hand with an elaborate display. In the complete darkness of the crypt, it illuminated her face with an eerie green glow as she examined the target date on the unit.

"What the hell is that?" Mayor knew he was whispering too loud again. "They told us that the EMP within the portal would fry anything we took through. No metal either or it's like being struck by lightning."

"It's a Denbora Control Plate," she said in an annoyed tone. "Mayor, say another word and I will gut you like a fish." She produced a long black dagger. The blade was double-edged and shined like glass in the green glow. He glanced from her face to the knife to the device in rapid sequence.

Mayor stayed quiet as Gina unbarred and opened the heavy iron door. He noticed it had been barred from the inside. *Inside a mausoleum.* It creeped him out. It was a good place for a fixed portal though.

They slipped quietly out. The only sound they made was disturbing a small drift of dry leaves behind the door.

"Just keep quiet and follow the damn protocol," Gina said to him as she began to move silently into the night. The city of Richmond Virginia glowed beyond the river below. "Just watch the events so you will know what to do next time through."

Mayor hated the protocol. He didn't believe in it. It relied on math that didn't add up. But he wanted to time travel even more. So, he followed the rules. *Expect the unexpected and remember.*

The first time into the past he had to follow *The Witness Protocol.* The protocol always bothered him because of the potential paradox of watching your mission outcome making sure your witnessing does not affect the outcome. He had to stay out of the way. And his later self would bring him his mission assignment. It was the last duty of every mission.

At least it had time built in for feelings of awe, *inspired by the beauty of the world before the desolation.* Gina obviously knew this. She led him to a bench and simply said, "Sit here. Keep to protocol. Back soon." With that, she touched a control on the small device and she became shadows and darkness. She was cloaked in black steam that seemed like it was drifting on an invisible breeze.

The lights of Richmond twinkled on the James River below. There were hints of music on the breeze. The air smelled beautiful. Mayor began to understand the more esoteric parts of the protocol. They had nothing to do with math. *Expect the unexpected.* He never expected that he'd feel like crying.

Mayor swallowed hard. He imagined the future. The crater that was once Richmond that had turned into a radioactive lake that the James River filled in. It had to be stopped. He knew his part in stopping it would be critical. *He had to follow the protocol.*

***

He sat on the bench for almost an hour. His mind raced in the beginning. Then he slowly calmed. A realization occurred to him. He intellectually understood the foundation principle of an *absolute past*. He had one that would always be his. The part that didn't make sense was that he was there to observe events of his future, in order to prepare for it. He would watch his future self to know and understand the outcomes of that important event. Watch himself, so that future self will remember and be prepared for the critical event. The Witness Protocol.

Roll with it.

When the portal opened inside another mausoleum ten meters directly in front of him, the light bled around the door and blinded him as the figure stepped through. He was wearing 27th century body armor complete with a helmet, carrying a temporal scanner and a large, old, beat up briefcase.

"You'll need this," the figure said as he dropped the case on the bench next to him. He retreated through the portal before it closed. Mayor glimpsed a platform of some kind, an oil rig maybe? Silently, the portal closed, leaving another door shaped spot in his vision. He had to blink it away.

Before his vision normalized, he heard Gina's voice. "About damn time." It was husky. Like she had been smoking all forty years of her life.

The shadow of an adjacent tree dissolved and Gina emerged from hiding.

"Wait." Mayor snatched the case before she could reach it. It was covered in dirt. Fresh earth. "This isn't protocol." He hugged it to his chest.

"Listen, Mayor." Gina sounded impatient. "Just unlock and open the case."

"How?" It had a classic six-digit combination lock. When he touched it, it lit so he could see it. "What's the combination?"

"Mayor, don't be stupid. That was you that just dropped it off." Gina scanned the area. "Don't you get it. You'll survive. That was you, post-event, making sure you could do your job. Bringing you what you forgot. Or didn't know to bring. Now open the case."

"How come the electronics didn't get fried?" he asked as he entered his mom's birthday and the case clicked open. He looked up before he opened it. Gina was gone.

The case had three packages inside, wrapped in plain brown paper. The smallest had, *"Open me first, dumbass."* written on it.

It was a thick bundle of worthless cash. *I am a dumbass,* he thought. *It's not worthless here. How could I not remember that?*

The next package was marked, *"Second, dipshit."* It didn't help to see that it was his own handwriting.

It was a glasses case. *I don't wear glasses,* he thought.

On the inside of the case was written, *"Just put them on now you idiot."* They were wraparound sunglasses.

When he put them on, they activated. They were obviously night-vision, but they were more than that. Letters appeared on the last package that were not visible earlier.

"Don't trust Gina. She's a liar. Open me fast and get ready to run."

Mayor tore open the package, crumbled the paper and put it into his coat pocket. It was a loaded handgun. A Glock 17 in perfectly preserved condition.

He glanced up and around. In the cemetery, the glasses allowed him to see a dozen figures drifting toward him.

They all looked like grim reapers as he could see blades of various kinds in their hands.

Mayor ran.

The Heads-Up Display (HUD) in these glasses were amazing. It somehow increased his peripheral vision. It increased the visual resolution of everything. He could now read distant road signs. It indicated his exact location in lat/longs to one centimeter, as well as direction and elevation.

Most importantly, it highlighted all the people that were in active camouflage.

It also had a recommended path to run. As he rounded a corner, he flinched at the sound of a gunshot behind him. He glanced over his shoulder, seeing all the followers stop and look about. Someone grabbed him and easily redirected him into another mausoleum that went into the hillside. His wrist with the Glock was pinned, and a hand went over his mouth.

"Silence, dumbass," whispered the same man that had brought the briefcase.

Mayor's eyes were wide with the realization that it was his future self. The mausoleum where they hid did not have a solid door. There were only bars, which allowed them to hear and watch the pursuers as they ran by.

"Shhhhh…" was whispered in his ear. Mayor stayed frozen. In his mind, the protocol echoed *TRUST YOURSELF*. It had an all new meaning now.

They did not move for what seemed like hours, but his HUD said it was only seven minutes. The hands released him as footsteps could be heard on the cinder path just opposite the doorway. A single grim reaper stopped and turned to face the doorway.

"Clear," was all the reaper said. The black steam seemed to dissipate and the camouflage shadows dissolved. It was another Mayor. A much older Mayor. He was wearing jeans and a brown tweed blazer over a black Oxford shirt. His graying hair was pulled back into a ponytail and he had a long beard.

"I'll see you when it's done," the third Mayor said as he produced a cigar and matchbook from his jacket. He then lit it with a wooden match.

They didn't move as they watched him stroll away into the cemetery.

"I…" Mayor One began, but Mayor Two interrupted him pulling off his helmet.

"The entire protocol is wrong. It was an intentional lie. We found that out after the Paradox was over. You… we caused the Witness Paradox. We also discovered that time travel is impossible. We were right all along, the math didn't add up. Einstein was right. There is no such thing as time. It's all an illusion." Mayor Two opened the bars and casually began to walk in the direction they came from.

"But…"

"There is only now." It was like he was reciting a well-practiced speech. "Now is the intersection between the past and future. Now is so thin it doesn't exist."

"I'm hungry," Mayor One said, thinking, *I am going to say some random shit to throw him off.*

"Saying random shit will not throw me off." Mayor Two looked over and smiled then. "For being such a dumbass you really are a genius."

"I really am hungry."

"I know. It's what starts the entire paradox. Try the toast. Leave a huge tip."

They crested a knoll to see two vehicles in the parking area. A blue 1970 Dodge Dart with a black vinyl top and a black spaceship resting on three legs.

As they quickly moved along, Mayor Two continued, "Directions to the Third Street Diner are in the HUD. Be careful with the Prof's car." With that Mayor Two tucked his helmet under his arm and entered the elevator under the ship. He waved as the doors slid closed.

Mayor went to wave back when he realized he still had the gun in his hand. He put it in his coat pocket and climbed into the car.

The car was in pristine condition. The keys were in the ignition. Even though the windows were all down, he could still smell the faint, sweet scent of cigars.

It started right up. The motor purred like it was new. He slowly left the cemetery and followed the HUD toward downtown.

***

Mayor parked at the curb in the street. The diner was on the corner, and about half a dozen people stood out front smoking cigarettes, even though it was 3:30AM.

As he walked up the sidewalk, he could smell bacon. *REAL BACON.*

There were four women and one man outside. The women wore very little, especially on a cold October night. The man with his back to Mayor wore a familiar brown tweed jacket and jeans. His ponytail went halfway down his back. The women were laughing at something he said. He never turned around as he puffed his cigar.

The diner was busy for the late hour. He could not help but stare at the waitress as she walked toward him. He had read about obese people but had never seen one his entire life. Her smile was bright.

"Sit anywhere you like, hon. The last booth is still open. Plenty of room at the counter," she said.

"Thanks, I'll take the booth." Mayor moved to the last booth. A small hall led past it to the bathrooms. He sat with his back to the wall.

The waitress was right behind him and poured coffee without asking. "Need a menu, or you know what you want, hon?"

"Eggs, and hash browns with extra bacon, please," he said. "And toast!"

"I love me decisive men." She winked at him in a near cartoon flirt.

The coffee was amazing. The breakfast came quickly and Mayor was impressed most by the toast. Real butter was all they said it would be and more.

Mayor didn't notice the diner had gotten quiet until he was popping the last bite of toast into his mouth.

Looking up, there was a girl standing with her back to him. Her arm was extended with a gun aiming directly at his older self's face.

"You think you're so smart." She glanced over her shoulder at someone in the next booth. "Not smart enough…" It was Gina. A much younger twenty-something Gina. Not the forty-something Gina that brought him here.

Mayor didn't think before he reacted. He had to protect his future self. He drew his Glock and fired a single shot at the girl, striking her in the back of the head. She collapsed like a puppet that had its strings cut.

The room was silent for only a moment.

"NOOOooo…" It was a scream from the forty-something Gina. She turned on Mayor One and raised her own gun. A massive stainless-steel revolver.

Before she could draw a bead on mayor, a baseball bat came down on her wrist, breaking it. Yet another Mayor held the bat.

"How can this be?" She sobbed. "I didn't die. I'm here. I remember killing him. You watched." Gina pointed at his face.

"In physics," the old Mayor said, "the observer effect is the theory that simply observing a situation or phenomenon necessarily changes that phenomenon."

"Time is an illusion," Mayor One said quietly.

Fourteen people stared. He realized everyone in the diner was from the future. One by one their active camouflage deactivated, and they were ALL Mayors. *But if it was true that there was only now.*

"We are not traveling in time," Mayor said. "It's always now. Even here. We have proof. This changes everything."

Mayor pointed the Glock at the dead twenty-something Gina.

***

Mayor One stood on the sidewalk lighting his first cigar that was given to him by his elder self. He could not watch his other selves load the body onto the ship. It was unnerving.

"The Witness Paradox is true," Gina said to elder Mayor as she cradled her wrist. "You'll never stop the coming disaster now, you bastard! I'll tell them what you did. You won't get away with this!"

"The coming disaster? It has not happened yet. Not here. All we can do is find the right… now," he replied. "There is no time travel. The portals don't travel in time. They go to parallel universes." Mayor One walked away into the night. "But we cannot allow anyone to know this. It will create panic, not purpose."

The ship rose silently into the sky. As the shadows enveloped the elder Mayor, he dissapeared into the night.

Mayor One reentered the diner to find the sleeping waitress in the first booth. He would sedate her on the next time through. He slid half the bundle of cash into her apron pocket, whispering, "Sorry about the mess." There was not too much blood.

He turned to watch Gina as she stood on the sidewalk, suffering in her realization. She was staring absently back at him in the empty diner when a man in 27th-century body armor appeared from the shadows and spoke.

"Witness this." The silent weapon's bullet entered her head but didn't exit. The man sifted through her pockets and came up with her Denbora Control Plate. He tossed it to Mayor One. "Now you can get started."

Mayor smiled as he left the diner. All signs of violence were gone. He was the only witness.

He climbed into the car and went in search of more cigars.

ABOUT THE AUTHORS

If you want to contact a specific author, please email
info@tannhauserpress.com.

The Writers Group, Copyright © 2018
by Martin Wilsey
Last Resort, Copyright © 2018
by Ricardo Garcia
Timely Saviors, Copyright © 2018
by Al Carroll
Clever Cosmic Joke, Copyright © 2018
by Scott A. Ceier
Let's Kill John A. , Copyright © 2018
by Jeffrey C. Jacobs
Weaponizing Time, Copyright © 2018
by Cameron E. A. Smith
Historinaut, Copyright © 2018
by Vincent Scarsella
Yahweh Project, Copyright © 2016
by Robert J. Aamoth
Screams of the Hypes, Copyright © 2018
by Terrence E. Zavecz
The Witness Paradox, Copyright © 2018
by Martin Wilsey

ACKNOWLEDEMENTS

In addition to the individual contributing authors, I would like to thank Jessica Johnson for all her help in the production of this anthology.

245

www.ingramcontent.com/pod-product-compliance
Lightning Source LLC
Chambersburg PA
CBHW060356310726
48976CB00003B/836